THE WORLD OF BEATRIX POTTER TREASURY™

FAVOURITE ✻ ORIGINAL PETER RABBIT™ TALES

THE ORIGINAL AND AUTHORIZED EDITION
BY **BEATRIX POTTER**

With new plates from the original illustrations

F. WARNE & C°

CLB

Colour Library Books

The reproductions in this book have been made using the most advanced electronic scanning methods from new transparencies of Beatrix Potter's original watercolours. The drawings now are reproduced with a quality and degree of authenticity never before attainable in print.

This edition published exclusively for Colour Library Books by
FREDERICK WARNE
Published by the Penguin Group
Penguin Books Ltd, 27 Wrights Lane, London W8 5TZ, England
Penguin Books USA Inc., 375 Hudson Street, New York, N.Y. 10014, USA
Penguin Books Australia Ltd, Ringwood, Victoria, Australia
Penguin Books Canada Ltd, 10 Alcorn Avenue, Toronto, Ontario, Canada M4V 3B2
Penguin Books (N.Z.) Ltd, 182-190 Wairau Road, Auckland 10 New Zealand

Penguin Books Ltd, Registered Offices: Harmondsworth, Middlesex, England

This edition first published by Frederick Warne & Co. 1996
3 5 7 9 10 8 6 4 2

This edition copyright © Frederick Warne & Co., 1996
New reproductions of Beatrix Potter's book illustrations copyright © Frederick Warne & Co., 1987
Original copyright in text and illustrations © Frederick Warne & Co., 1902, 1904, 1905, 1906,
1907, 1908, 1909, 1912, 1913

Frederick Warne & Co. is the owner of all rights, copyrights and trademarks in the Beatrix Potter
character names and illustrations.

ISBN 0 7232 4352 2

Printed and bound in Great Britain by William Clowes Limited, Beccles and London

CONTENTS

THE TALE OF
PETER RABBIT

ONCE upon a time there were four little Rabbits, and their names were—

Flopsy,
Mopsy,
Cotton-tail,
and Peter.

They lived with their Mother in a sand-bank, underneath the root of a very big fir-tree.

'NOW, my dears,' said old Mrs. Rabbit one morning, 'you may go into the fields or down the lane, but don't go into Mr. McGregor's garden: your Father had an accident there; he was put in a pie by Mrs. McGregor.'

'NOW run along, and don't get into mischief. I am going out.'

THEN old Mrs. Rabbit took a basket and her umbrella, and went through the wood to the baker's. She bought a loaf of brown bread and five currant buns.

FLOPSY, Mopsy, and Cotton-tail, who were good little bunnies, went down the lane to gather blackberries:

BUT Peter, who was very naughty, ran straight away to Mr. McGregor's garden, and squeezed under the gate!

FIRST he ate some lettuces and some French beans; and then he ate some radishes;

AND then, feeling rather sick, he went to look for some parsley.

BUT round the end of a cucumber frame, whom should he meet but Mr. McGregor!

MR. McGREGOR was on his hands and knees planting out young cabbages, but he jumped up and ran after Peter, waving a rake and calling out, 'Stop thief!'

PETER was most dreadfully frightened; he rushed all over the garden, for he had forgotten the way back to the gate.

He lost one of his shoes among the cabbages, and the other shoe amongst the potatoes.

AFTER losing them, he ran on four legs and went faster, so that I think he might have got away altogether if he had not unfortunately run into a gooseberry net, and got caught by the large buttons on his jacket. It was a blue jacket with brass buttons, quite new.

PETER gave himself up for lost, and shed big tears; but his sobs were overheard by some friendly sparrows, who flew to him in great excitement, and implored him to exert himself.

MR. McGREGOR came up with a sieve, which he intended to pop upon the top of Peter; but Peter wriggled out just in time, leaving his jacket behind him.

AND rushed into the tool-shed, and jumped into a can. It would have been a beautiful thing to hide in, if it had not had so much water in it.

MR. McGREGOR was quite sure that Peter was somewhere in the tool-shed, perhaps hidden underneath a flower-pot. He began to turn them over carefully, looking under each.

Presently Peter sneezed— 'Kertyschoo!' Mr. McGregor was after him in no time.

AND tried to put his foot upon Peter, who jumped out of a window, upsetting three plants. The window was too small for Mr. McGregor, and he was tired of running after Peter. He went back to his work.

PETER sat down to rest; he was out of breath and trembling with fright, and he had not the least idea which way to go. Also he was very damp with sitting in that can.

After a time he began to wander about, going lippity—lippity—not very fast, and looking all round.

HE found a door in a wall; but it was locked, and there was no room for a fat little rabbit to squeeze underneath.

An old mouse was running in and out over the stone door-step, carrying peas and beans to her family in the wood. Peter asked her the way to the gate, but she had such a large pea in her mouth that she could not answer. She only shook her head at him. Peter began to cry.

THEN he tried to find his way straight across the garden, but he became more and more puzzled. Presently, he came to a pond where Mr. McGregor filled his water-cans. A white cat was staring at some gold-fish, she sat very, very still, but now and then the tip of her tail twitched as if it were alive. Peter thought it best to go away without speaking to her; he had heard about cats from his cousin, little Benjamin Bunny.

HE went back towards the tool-shed, but suddenly, quite close to him, he heard the noise of a hoe—scr-r-ritch, scratch, scratch, scritch. Peter scuttered underneath the bushes. But presently, as nothing happened, he came out, and climbed upon a wheel-barrow and peeped over. The first thing that he saw was Mr. McGregor hoeing onions. His back was turned towards Peter, and beyond him was the gate!

PETER got down very quietly off the wheelbarrow, and started running as fast as he could go, along a straight walk behind some black-currant bushes.

Mr. McGregor caught sight of him at the corner, but Peter did not care. He slipped underneath the gate, and was safe at last in the wood outside the garden.

MR. McGREGOR hung up the little jacket and the shoes for a scare-crow to frighten the blackbirds.

PETER never stopped running or looked behind him till he got home to the big fir-tree.

He was so tired that he flopped down upon the nice soft sand on the floor of the rabbit-hole and shut his eyes. His mother was busy cooking; she wondered what he had done with his clothes. It was the second little jacket and pair of shoes that Peter had lost in a fortnight !

I AM sorry to say that Peter was not very well during the evening.

His mother put him to bed, and made some camomile tea; and she gave a dose of it to Peter!

'One table-spoonful to be taken at bed-time.'

BUT Flopsy, Mopsy, and Cotton-tail had bread and milk and blackberries for supper.

THE TALE OF
BENJAMIN BUNNY

For the children of Sawrey
from
Old Mr. Bunny

ONE morning a little rabbit sat on a bank.

He pricked his ears and listened to the trit-trot, trit-trot of a pony.

A gig was coming along the road; it was driven by Mr. McGregor, and beside him sat Mrs. McGregor in her best bonnet.

AS soon as they had passed, little Benjamin Bunny slid down into the road, and set off—with a hop, skip and a jump—to call upon his relations, who lived in the wood at the back of Mr. McGregor's garden.

THAT wood was full of rabbit holes; and in the neatest sandiest hole of all, lived Benjamin's aunt and his cousins—Flopsy, Mopsy, Cotton-tail and Peter.

Old Mrs. Rabbit was a widow; she earned her living by knitting rabbit-wool mittens and muffetees (I once bought a pair at a bazaar). She also sold herbs, and rosemary tea, and rabbit-tobacco (which is what *we* call lavender).

LITTLE Benjamin did not very much want to see his Aunt.

He came round the back of the fir-tree, and nearly tumbled upon the top of his Cousin Peter.

PETER was sitting by himself. He looked poorly, and was dressed in a red cotton pocket-handkerchief.

'Peter,'—said little Benjamin, in a whisper—'who has got your clothes?'

PETER replied—'The scarecrow in Mr. McGregor's garden,' and described how he had been chased about the garden, and had dropped his shoes and coat.

Little Benjamin sat down beside his cousin, and assured him that Mr. McGregor had gone out in a gig, and Mrs. McGregor also; and certainly for the day, because she was wearing her best bonnet.

PETER said he hoped that it would rain.

At this point, old Mrs. Rabbit's voice was heard inside the rabbit hole, calling—'Cotton-tail! Cotton-tail! fetch some more camomile!'

Peter said he thought he might feel better if he went for a walk.

THEY went away hand in hand, and got upon the flat top of the wall at the bottom of the wood. From here they looked down into Mr. McGregor's garden. Peter's coat and shoes were plainly to be seen upon the scarecrow, topped with an old tam-o-shanter of Mr. McGregor's.

LITTLE Benjamin said, 'It spoils people's clothes to squeeze under a gate; the proper way to get in, is to climb down a pear tree.'

Peter fell down head first; but it was of no consequence, as the bed below was newly raked and quite soft.

IT had been sown with lettuces.

They left a great many odd little foot-marks all over the bed, especially little Benjamin, who was wearing clogs.

LITTLE Benjamin said that the first thing to be done was to get back Peter's clothes, in order that they might be able to use the pocket-handkerchief.

They took them off the scarecrow. There had been rain during the night; there was water in the shoes, and the coat was somewhat shrunk.

Benjamin tried on the tam-o-shanter, but it was too big for him.

THEN he suggested that they should fill the pocket-handkerchief with onions, as a little present for his Aunt.

Peter did not seem to be enjoying himself; he kept hearing noises.

BENJAMIN, on the contrary, was perfectly at home, and ate a lettuce leaf. He said that he was in the habit of coming to the garden with his father to get lettuces for their Sunday dinner.

(The name of little Benjamin's papa was old Mr. Benjamin Bunny.)

The lettuces certainly were very fine.

PETER did not eat anything; he said he should like to go home. Presently he dropped half the onions.

LITTLE Benjamin said that it was not possible to get
back up the pear-tree, with a load of vegetables. He led
the way boldly towards the other end of the garden. They
went along a little walk on planks, under a sunny red-brick
wall.

The mice sat on their door-steps cracking cherry-stones,
they winked at Peter Rabbit and little Benjamin Bunny.

PRESENTLY Peter let the pocket-handkerchief go again.

THEY got amongst flower-pots, and frames and tubs; Peter heard noises worse than ever, his eyes were as big as lollypops!

He was a step or two in front of his cousin, when he suddenly stopped.

THIS is what those little rabbits saw round that corner!

Little Benjamin took one look, and then, in half a minute less than no time, he hid himself and Peter and the onions underneath a large basket....

THE cat got up and stretched herself, and came and sniffed at the basket.

Perhaps she liked the smell of onions!

Anyway, she sat down upon the top of the basket.

SHE sat there for *five hours*.

* * * * *

I cannot draw you a picture of Peter and Benjamin underneath the basket, because it was quite dark, and because the smell of onions was fearful; it made Peter Rabbit and little Benjamin cry.

The sun got round behind the wood, and it was quite late in the afternoon; but still the cat sat upon the basket.

AT length there was a pitter-patter, pitter-patter, and some bits of mortar fell from the wall above.

The cat looked up and saw old Mr. Benjamin Bunny prancing along the top of the wall of the upper terrace.

He was smoking a pipe of rabbit-tobacco, and had a little switch in his hand.

He was looking for his son.

OLD Mr. Bunny had no opinion whatever of cats.

He took a tremendous jump off the top of the wall on to the top of the cat, and cuffed it off the basket, and kicked it into the green-house, scratching off a handful of fur.

The cat was too much surprised to scratch back.

WHEN old Mr. Bunny had driven the cat into the green-house, he locked the door.

Then he came back to the basket and took out his son Benjamin by the ears, and whipped him with the little switch.

Then he took out his nephew Peter.

THEN he took out the handkerchief of onions, and marched out of the garden.

31

WHEN Mr. McGregor returned about half an hour later, he observed several things which perplexed him.

It looked as though some person had been walking all over the garden in a pair of clogs—only the foot-marks were too ridiculously little!

Also he could not understand how the cat could have managed to shut herself up *inside* the greenhouse, locking the door upon the *outside.*

WHEN Peter got home, his mother forgave him, because she was so glad to see that he had found his shoes and coat. Cotton-tail and Peter folded up the pocket-handkerchief, and old Mrs. Rabbit strung up the onions and hung them from the kitchen ceiling, with the bunches of herbs and the rabbit-tobacco.

THE TALE OF
THE FLOPSY BUNNIES

For all little friends
of
Mr. McGregor and Peter and Benjamin

IT is said that the effect of eating too much lettuce is 'soporific.'

I have never felt sleepy after eating lettuces ; but then *I* am not a rabbit.

They certainly had a very soporific effect upon the Flopsy Bunnies !

WHEN Benjamin Bunny grew up, he married his Cousin Flopsy. They had a large family, and they were very improvident and cheerful.

I do not remember the separate names of their children; they were generally called the 'Flopsy Bunnies.'

AS there was not always quite enough to eat,—Benjamin used to borrow cabbages from Flopsy's brother, Peter Rabbit, who kept a nursery garden.

SOMETIMES Peter Rabbit had no cabbages to spare.

WHEN this happened, the Flopsy Bunnies went across the field to a rubbish heap, in the ditch outside Mr. McGregor's garden.

MR. McGREGOR'S rubbish heap was a mixture. There were jam pots and paper bags, and mountains of chopped grass from the mowing machine (which always tasted oily), and some rotten vegetable marrows and an old boot or two. One day—oh joy!— there were a quantity of overgrown lettuces, which had 'shot' into flower.

THE Flopsy Bunnies simply stuffed lettuces. By degrees, one after another, they were overcome with slumber, and lay down in the mown grass.

Benjamin was not so much overcome as his children. Before going to sleep he was sufficiently wide awake to put a paper bag over his head to keep off the flies.

THE little Flopsy Bunnies slept delightfully in the warm sun. From the lawn beyond the garden came the distant clacketty sound of the mowing machine. The blue-bottles buzzed about the wall, and a little old mouse picked over the rubbish among the jam pots.

(I can tell you her name, she was called Thomasina Tittlemouse, a woodmouse with a long tail.)

SHE rustled across the paper bag, and awakened Benjamin Bunny.

The mouse apologized profusely, and said that she knew Peter Rabbit.

WHILE she and Benjamin were talking, close under the wall, they heard a heavy tread above their heads; and suddenly Mr. McGregor emptied out a sackful of lawn mowings right upon the top of the sleeping Flopsy Bunnies! Benjamin shrank down under his paper bag. The mouse hid in a jam pot.

THE little rabbits smiled sweetly in their sleep under the shower of grass; they did not awake because the lettuces had been so soporific.

They dreamt that their mother Flopsy was tucking them up in a hay bed.

Mr. McGregor looked down after emptying his sack. He saw some funny little brown tips of ears sticking up through the lawn mowings. He stared at them for some time.

PRESENTLY a fly set-
tled on one of them and
it moved.

Mr. McGregor climbed
down on to the rubbish
heap—

'One, two, three, four!
five! six leetle rabbits!' said
he as he dropped them into
his sack. The Flopsy Bun-
nies dreamt that their
mother was turning them
over in bed. They stirred a
little in their sleep, but still
they did not wake up.

MR. McGREGOR tied
up the sack and left it
on the wall.

He went to put away the
mowing machine.

WHILE he was gone,
Mrs. Flopsy Bunny
(who had remained at
home) came across the field.

She looked suspiciously at
the sack and wondered
where everybody was?

THEN the mouse came out of her jam pot, and Benjamin took the paper bag off his head, and they told the doleful tale.

Benjamin and Flopsy were in despair, they could not undo the string.

But Mrs. Tittlemouse was a resourceful person. She nibbled a hole in the bottom corner of the sack.

THE little rabbits were pulled out and pinched to wake them.

Their parents stuffed the empty sack with three rotten vegetable marrows, an old blacking-brush and two decayed turnips.

THEN they all hid under a bush and watched for Mr. McGregor.

MR. McGREGOR came back and picked up the sack, and carried it off.

He carried it hanging down, as if it were rather heavy.

The Flopsy Bunnies followed at a safe distance.

THEY watched him go into his house.

And then they crept up to the window to listen.

MR. McGREGOR threw down the sack on the stone floor in a way that would have been extremely painful to the Flopsy Bunnies, if they had happened to have been inside it.

They could hear him drag his chair on the flags, and chuckle—

'One, two, three, four, five, six leetle rabbits!' said Mr. McGregor.

'Eh? What's that? What have they been spoiling now?' enquired Mrs. McGregor.

'One, two, three, four, five, six leetle fat rabbits!' repeated Mr. McGregor, counting on his fingers—'one, two, three—'

'Don't you be silly; what do you mean, you silly old man?'

'In the sack! one, two, three, four, five, six!' replied Mr. McGregor.

(The youngest Flopsy Bunny got upon the window-sill.)

MRS. McGREGOR took hold of the sack and felt it. She said she could feel six, but they must be *old* rabbits, because they were so hard and all different shapes.

'Not fit to eat; but the skins will do fine to line my old cloak.'

'Line your old cloak?' shouted Mr. McGregor—'I shall sell them and buy myself baccy!'

'Rabbit tobacco! I shall skin them and cut off their heads.'

MRS. McGREGOR untied the sack and put her hand inside.

When she felt the vegetables she became very very angry. She said that Mr. McGregor had 'done it a purpose.'

AND Mr. McGregor was very angry too. One of the rotten marrows came flying through the kitchen window, and hit the youngest Flopsy Bunny.

It was rather hurt.

THEN Benjamin and Flopsy thought that it was time to go home.

SO Mr. McGregor did not get his tobacco, and Mrs. McGregor did not get her rabbit skins.

But next Christmas Thomasina Tittlemouse got a present of enough rabbit-wool to make herself a cloak and a hood, and a handsome muff and a pair of warm mittens.

THE TALE OF
MR. TOD

For Francis William of Ulva
— someday!

I HAVE made many books about well-behaved people. Now, for a change, I am going to make a story about two disagreeable people, called Tommy Brock and Mr. Tod.

Nobody could call Mr. Tod 'nice.' The rabbits could not bear him; they could smell him half a mile off. He was of a wandering habit and he had foxey whiskers; they never knew where he would be next.

One day he was living in a stick-house in the coppice, causing terror to the family of old Mr. Benjamin Bouncer. Next day he moved into a pollard willow near the lake, frightening the wild ducks and the water rats.

In winter and early spring he might generally be found in an earth amongst the rocks at the top of Bull Banks, under Oatmeal Crag.

He had half a dozen houses, but he was seldom at home.

The houses were not always empty when Mr. Tod moved *out;* because sometimes Tommy Brock moved *in;* (without asking leave).

Tommy Brock was a short bristly fat waddling person with a grin; he grinned all over his face. He was not nice in his habits. He ate wasp nests and frogs and worms; and he waddled about by moonlight, digging things up.

His clothes were very dirty; and as he slept in the day-time, he always went to bed in his boots. And the bed which he went to bed in, was generally Mr. Tod's.

Now Tommy Brock did occasionally eat rabbit-pie; but it was only very little young ones occasionally, when other food was really scarce. He was friendly with old Mr. Bouncer; they agreed in disliking the wicked otters and Mr. Tod; they often talked over that painful subject.

Old Mr. Bouncer was stricken in years. He sat in the spring sunshine outside the burrow, in a muffler; smoking a pipe of rabbit tobacco.

He lived with his son Benjamin Bunny and his daughter-in-law Flopsy, who had a young family. Old Mr. Bouncer was in charge of the family that afternoon, because Benjamin and Flopsy had gone out. The little rabbit-babies were just old enough to open their blue eyes and kick. They lay in a fluffy bed of rabbit wool and hay, in a shallow burrow, separate from the main rabbit hole. To tell the truth—old Mr. Bouncer had forgotten them.

He sat in the sun, and conversed cordially with Tommy Brock, who was passing through the wood with a sack and a little spud which he used for digging, and some mole traps. He complained bitterly about the scarcity of pheasants' eggs, and accused Mr. Tod of poaching them. And the otters had cleared off all the frogs while he was asleep in winter—'I have not had a good square meal for a fortnight, I am living on pig-nuts. I shall have to turn vegetarian and eat my own tail!' said Tommy Brock.

It was not much of a joke, but it tickled old Mr. Bouncer; because Tommy Brock was so fat and stumpy and grinning.

So old Mr. Bouncer laughed; and pressed Tommy Brock to come inside, to taste a slice of seed-cake and 'a glass of my daughter Flopsy's cowslip wine.' Tommy Brock squeezed himself into the rabbit hole with alacrity.

Then old Mr. Bouncer smoked another pipe, and gave Tommy Brock a cabbage leaf cigar which was so very strong that it made Tommy Brock grin more than ever; and the smoke filled the burrow. Old Mr. Bouncer coughed and laughed; and Tommy Brock puffed and grinned.

And Mr. Bouncer laughed and coughed, and shut his eyes because of the cabbage smoke . . . .

When Flopsy and Benjamin came back—old Mr. Bouncer woke up. Tommy Brock and all the young rabbit-babies had disappeared!

Mr. Bouncer would not confess that he had admitted anybody into the rabbit hole. But the smell of badger was undeniable; and there were round heavy footmarks in the sand. He was in disgrace; Flopsy wrung her ears, and slapped him.

Benjamin Bunny set off at once after Tommy Brock.

There was not much difficulty in tracking him; he had left his footmark and gone slowly up the winding footpath through the wood. Here he had rooted up the moss and wood sorrel. There he had dug quite a deep hole for dog darnel; and had set a mole trap. A little stream crossed the way. Benjamin skipped lightly over dry-foot; the badger's heavy steps showed plainly in the mud.

The path led to a part of the thicket where the trees had been cleared; there were leafy oak stumps, and a sea of blue hyacinths—but the smell that made Benjamin stop, was *not* the smell of flowers!

Mr. Tod's stick house was before him and, for once,

Mr. Tod was at home. There was not only a foxey flavour in proof of it—there was smoke coming out of the broken pail that served as a chimney.

Benjamin Bunny sat up, staring; his whiskers twitched. Inside the stick house somebody dropped a plate, and said something. Benjamin stamped his foot, and bolted.

He never stopped till he came to the other side of the wood. Apparently Tommy Brock had turned the same way. Upon the top of the wall, there were again the marks of badger; and some ravellings of a sack had caught on a briar.

Benjamin climbed over the wall, into a meadow. He found another mole trap newly set; he was still upon the track of Tommy Brock. It was getting late in the afternoon. Other rabbits were coming out to enjoy the evening air. One of them in a blue coat by himself, was busily hunting for dandelions.—'Cousin Peter! Peter Rabbit, Peter Rabbit!' shouted Benjamin Bunny.

The blue coated rabbit sat up with pricked ears—

'Whatever is the matter, Cousin Benjamin? Is it a cat? or John Stoat Ferret?'

'No, no, no! He's bagged my family—Tommy Brock —in a sack—have you seen him?'

'Tommy Brock? how many, Cousin Benjamin?'

'Seven, Cousin Peter, and all of them twins! Did he come this way? Please tell me quick!'

'Yes, yes; not ten minutes since.... he said they were *caterpillars;* I did think they were kicking rather hard, for caterpillars.'

'Which way? which way has he gone, Cousin Peter?'

'He had a sack with something 'live in it; I watched him set a mole trap. Let me use my mind, Cousin Benjamin; tell me from the beginning.' Benjamin did so.

'My Uncle Bouncer has displayed a lamentable want of discretion for his years;' said Peter reflectively, 'but there are two hopeful circumstances. Your family is alive and kicking; and Tommy Brock has had refreshment. He will probably go to sleep, and keep them for breakfast.' 'Which way?' 'Cousin Benjamin, compose yourself. I know very well which way. Because Mr. Tod was at home in the stick-house he has gone to Mr. Tod's other house, at the top of Bull Banks. I partly know, because he offered to leave any message at Sister Cottontail's; he said he would be passing.' (Cottontail had married a black rabbit, and gone to live on the hill).

Peter hid his dandelions, and accompanied the afflicted parent, who was all of a twitter. They crossed several fields

53

and began to climb the hill; the tracks of Tommy Brock were plainly to be seen. He seemed to have put down the sack every dozen yards, to rest.

' 'He must be very puffed; we are close behind him, by the scent. What a nasty person!' said Peter.

The sunshine was still warm and slanting on the hill pastures. Half way up, Cottontail was sitting in her doorway, with four or five half-grown little rabbits playing about her; one black and the others brown.

Cottontail had seen Tommy Brock passing in the distance. Asked whether her husband was at home she replied that Tommy Brock had rested twice while she watched him.

He had nodded, and pointed to the sack, and seemed

doubled up with laughing.—'Come away, Peter; he will be cooking them; come quicker!' said Benjamin Bunny.

They climbed up and up;—'He was at home; I saw his black ears peeping out of the hole.' 'They live too near the rocks to quarrel with their neighbours. Come on, Cousin Benjamin!'

When they came near the wood at the top of Bull Banks, they went cautiously. The trees grew amongst heaped up rocks; and there, beneath a crag—Mr. Tod had made one of his homes. It was at the top of a steep bank ; the rocks and bushes overhung it. The rabbits crept up carefully, listening and peeping.

This house was something between a cave, a prison, and a tumble-down pig-stye. There was a strong door, which was shut and locked.

The setting sun made the window panes glow like red flame; but the kitchen fire was not alight. It was neatly laid with dry sticks, as the rabbits could see, when they peeped through the window.

Benjamin sighed with relief.

But there were preparations upon the kitchen table which made him shudder. There was an immense empty pie-dish of blue willow pattern, and a large carving knife and fork, and a chopper.

At the other end of the table was a partly unfolded tablecloth, a plate, a tumbler, a knife and fork, salt-cellar, mustard and a chair—in short, preparations for one person's supper.

No person was to be seen, and no young rabbits. The kitchen was empty and silent; the clock had run down. Peter and Benjamin flattened their noses against the window, and stared into the dusk.

Then they scrambled round the rocks to the other side of the house. It was damp and smelly, and overgrown with thorns and briars.

The rabbits shivered in their shoes.

'Oh my poor rabbit babies! What a dreadful place; I shall never see them again!' sighed Benjamin.

They crept up to the bedroom window. It was closed and bolted like the kitchen. But there were signs that this window had been recently open; the cobwebs were disturbed, and there were fresh dirty footmarks upon the window-sill.

The room inside was so dark, that at first they could make out nothing; but they could hear a noise—a slow deep regular snoring grunt. And as their eyes became accustomed to the darkness, they perceived that somebody was asleep on

Mr. Tod's bed, curled up under the blanket.—'He has gone to bed in his boots,' whispered Peter.

Benjamin, who was all of a twitter, pulled Peter off the window-sill.

Tommy Brock's snores continued, grunty and regular from Mr. Tod's bed. Nothing could be seen of the young family.

The sun had set; an owl began to hoot in the wood. There were many unpleasant things lying about, that had much better have been buried; rabbit bones and skulls, and chickens' legs and other horrors. It was a shocking place, and very dark.

They went back to the front of the house, and tried in every way to move the bolt of the kitchen window. They tried to push up a rusty nail between the window sashes; but it was of no use, especially without a light.

They sat side by side outside the window, whispering and listening.

In half an hour the moon rose over the wood. It shone full and clear and cold, upon the house amongst the rocks, and in at the kitchen window. But alas, no little rabbit babies were to be seen!

The moonbeams twinkled on the carving knife and the pie dish, and made a path of brightness across the dirty floor.

The light showed a little door in a wall beside the kitchen fireplace—a little iron door belonging to a brick oven, of that old-fashioned sort that used to be heated with faggots of wood.

And presently at the same moment Peter and Benjamin noticed that whenever they shook the window—the little door opposite shook in answer. The young family were alive; shut up in the oven!

Benjamin was so excited that it was a mercy he did not awake Tommy Brock, whose snores continued solemnly in Mr. Tod's bed.

But there really was not very much comfort in the discovery. They could not open the window; and although the young family was alive—the little rabbits were quite incapable of letting themselves out; they were not old enough to crawl.

After much whispering, Peter and Benjamin decided to dig a tunnel. They began to burrow a yard or two lower down the bank. They hoped that they might be able to work between the large stones under the house; the kitchen floor was so dirty that it was impossible to say whether it was made of earth or flags.

They dug and dug for hours. They could not tunnel straight on account of stones; but by the end of the night they were under the kitchen floor. Benjamin was on his back, scratching upwards. Peter's claws were worn down; he was outside the tunnel, shuffling sand away. He called out that it was morning—sunrise; and that the jays were making a noise down below in the woods.

Benjamin Bunny came out of the dark tunnel, shaking the sand from his ears; he cleaned his face with his paws. Every minute the sun shone warmer on the top of the hill. In the valley there was a sea of white mist, with golden tops of trees showing through.

Again from the fields down below in the mist there came the angry cry of a jay—followed by the sharp yelping bark of a fox!

Then those two rabbits lost their heads completely. They did the most foolish thing that they could have done. They rushed into their short new tunnel, and hid themselves at the top end of it, under Mr. Tod's kitchen floor.

Mr. Tod was coming up Bull Banks, and he was in the very worst of tempers. First he had been upset by breaking the plate. It was his own fault; but it was a china plate, the last of the dinner service that had belonged to his grandmother, old Vixen Tod. Then the midges had been very bad.

And he had failed to catch a hen pheasant on her nest; and it had contained only five eggs, two of them addled. Mr. Tod had had an unsatisfactory night.

As usual, when out of humour, he determined to move house. First he tried the pollard willow, but it was damp; and the otters had left a dead fish near it. Mr. Tod likes nobody's leavings but his own.

He made his way up the hill; his temper was not improved by noticing unmistakable marks of badger. No one else grubs up the moss so wantonly as Tommy Brock.

Mr. Tod slapped his stick upon the earth and fumed; he guessed where Tommy Brock had gone to. He was further annoyed by the jay bird which followed him persistently. It flew from tree to tree and scolded, warning every rabbit within hearing that either a cat or a fox was coming up the plantation. Once when it flew screaming over his head—Mr. Tod snapped at it, and barked.

He approached his house very carefully, with a large rusty key. He sniffed and his whiskers bristled. The house was locked up, but Mr. Tod had his doubts whether it was empty. He turned the rusty key in the lock; the rabbits below could hear it. Mr. Tod opened the door cautiously and went in.

The sight that met Mr. Tod's eyes in Mr. Tod's kitchen made Mr. Tod furious. There was Mr. Tod's chair, and Mr. Tod's pie dish, and his knife and fork and mustard and salt cellar and his table-cloth that he had left folded up in the dresser—all set out for supper (or breakfast)—without doubt for that odious Tommy Brock.

There was a smell of fresh earth and dirty badger, which fortunately overpowered all smell of rabbit.

But what absorbed Mr. Tod's attention was a noise—a deep slow regular snoring grunting noise, coming from his own bed.

He peeped through the hinges of the half-open bedroom door. Then he turned and came out of the house in a hurry. His whiskers bristled and his coat-collar stood on end with rage.

For the next twenty minutes Mr. Tod kept creeping cautiously into the house, and retreating hurriedly out again. By degrees he ventured further in—right into the bedroom. When he was outside the house, he scratched up the earth with fury. But when he was inside—he did not like the look of Tommy Brock's teeth.

He was lying on his back with his mouth open, grinning from ear to ear. He snored peacefully and regularly; but one eye was not perfectly shut.

Mr. Tod came in and out of the bedroom. Twice he brought in his walking-stick, and once he brought in the coal-scuttle. But he thought better of it, and took them away.

When he came back after removing the coal-scuttle, Tommy Brock was lying a little more sideways; but he seemed even sounder asleep. He was an incurably indolent person; he was not in the least afraid of Mr. Tod; he was simply too lazy and comfortable to move.

Mr. Tod came back yet again into the bedroom with a clothes line. He stood a minute watching Tommy Brock and listening attentively to the snores. They were very loud indeed, but seemed quite natural.

Mr. Tod turned his back towards the bed, and undid the window. It creaked; he turned round with a jump. Tommy Brock, who had opened one eye—shut it hastily. The snores continued.

Mr. Tod's proceedings were peculiar, and rather uneasy, (because the bed was between the window and the door of the bedroom). He opened the window a little way, and pushed out the greater part of the clothes line on to the window sill. The rest of the line, with a hook at the end, remained in his hand.

Tommy Brock snored conscientiously. Mr. Tod stood and looked at him for a minute; then he left the room again.

Tommy Brock opened both eyes, and looked at the rope and grinned. There was a noise outside the window. Tommy Brock shut his eyes in a hurry.

Mr. Tod had gone out at the front door, and round to the back of the house. On the way, he stumbled over the rabbit burrow. If he had had any idea who was inside it, he would have pulled them out quickly.

His foot went through the tunnel nearly upon the top of Peter Rabbit and Benjamin, but fortunately he thought that it was some more of Tommy Brock's work.

He took up the coil of line from the sill, listened for a moment, and then tied the rope to a tree.

Tommy Brock watched him with one eye, through the window. He was puzzled.

Mr. Tod fetched a large heavy pailful of water from the spring, and staggered with it through the kitchen into his bedroom.

Tommy Brock snored industriously, with rather a snort.

Mr. Tod put down the pail beside the bed, took up the end of rope with the hook—hesitated, and looked at Tommy Brock. The snores were almost apoplectic; but the grin was not quite so big.

Mr Tod gingerly mounted a chair by the head of the bedstead. His legs were dangerously near to Tommy Brock's teeth.

He reached up and put the end of rope, with the hook, over the head of the tester bed, where the curtains ought to hang.

(Mr. Tod's curtains were folded up, and put away, owing to the house being unoccupied. So was the counterpane. Tommy Brock was covered with a blanket only.) Mr. Tod standing on the unsteady chair looked down upon him attentively; he really was a first prize sound sleeper!

It seemed as though nothing would waken him—not even the flapping rope across the bed.

Mr. Tod descended safely from the chair, and endeavoured to get up again with the pail of water. He intended to hang it from the hook, dangling over the head of Tommy Brock, in order to make a sort of shower-bath, worked by a string, through the window.

But naturally being a thin-legged person (though vindictive and sandy whiskered)—he was quite unable to lift the heavy weight to the level of the hook and rope. He very nearly overbalanced himself.

The snores became more and more apoplectic. One of Tommy Brock's hind legs twitched under the blanket, but still he slept on peacefully.

Mr. Tod and the pail descended from the chair without accident. After considerable thought, he emptied the water into a washbasin and jug. The empty pail was not too heavy for him; he slung it up wobbling over the head of Tommy Brock.

Surely there never was such a sleeper! Mr. Tod got up and down, down and up on the chair.

As he could not lift the whole pailful of water at once, he fetched a milk jug, and ladled quarts of water into the pail by degrees. The pail got fuller and fuller, and swung like a pendulum. Occasionally a drop splashed over; but still Tommy Brock snored regularly and never moved,—except one eye.

At last Mr. Tod's preparations were complete. The pail was full of water; the rope was tightly strained over the top of the bed, and across the window sill to the tree outside.

'It will make a great mess in my bedroom; but I could never sleep in that bed again without a spring cleaning of some sort,' said Mr. Tod.

Mr. Tod took a last look at the badger and softly left the room. He went out of the house, shutting the front door. The rabbits heard his footsteps over the tunnel.

He ran round behind the house, intending to undo the rope in order to let fall the pailful of water upon Tommy Brock—

'I will wake him up with an unpleasant surprise,' said Mr. Tod.

The moment he had gone, Tommy Brock got up in a hurry; he rolled Mr. Tod's dressing-gown into a bundle, put it into the bed beneath the pail of water instead of himself, and left the room also—grinning immensely.

He went into the kitchen, lighted the fire and boiled the kettle; for the moment he did not trouble himself to cook the baby rabbits.

When Mr. Tod got to the tree, he found that the weight and strain had dragged the knot so tight that it was past untying. He was obliged to gnaw it with his teeth. He chewed and gnawed for more than twenty minutes. At last the rope gave way with such a sudden jerk that it nearly pulled his teeth out, and quite knocked him over backwards.

Inside the house there was a great crash and splash, and the noise of a pail rolling over and over.

But no screams. Mr. Tod was mystified; he sat quite still, and listened attentively.

Then he peeped in at the window. The water was dripping from the bed, the pail had rolled into a corner.

In the middle of the bed under the blanket, was a wet flattened *something*— much dinged in, in the middle where the pail had caught it (as it were across the tummy). Its head was covered by the wet blanket and it was *not snoring any longer.*

There was nothing stirring, and no sound except the drip, drop, drop drip of water trickling from the mattress.

Mr. Tod watched it for half an hour; his eyes glistened.

Then he cut a caper, and became so bold that he even tapped at the window; but the bundle never moved.

Yes—there was no doubt about it—it had turned out even better than he had planned; the pail had hit poor old Tommy Brock, and killed him dead!

'I will bury that nasty person in the hole which he has dug. I will bring my bedding out, and dry it in the sun,' said Mr. Tod.

'I will wash the tablecloth and spread it on the grass in the sun to bleach. And the blanket must be hung up in the wind; and the bed must be thoroughly disinfected, and aired with a warming-pan; and warmed with a hot-water bottle.'

'I will get soft soap, and monkey soap, and all sorts of soap; and soda and scrubbing brushes; and persian powder; and carbolic to remove the smell. I must have a disinfecting. Perhaps I may have to burn sulphur.'

He hurried round the house to get a shovel from the kitchen—'First I will arrange the hole—then I will drag out that person in the blanket ...'

He opened the door....

Tommy Brock was sitting at Mr. Tod's kitchen table, pouring out tea from Mr. Tod's tea-pot into Mr. Tod's tea-cup. He was quite dry himself and grinning; and he threw the cup of scalding tea all over Mr. Tod.

Then Mr. Tod rushed upon Tommy Brock, and Tommy Brock grappled with Mr. Tod amongst the broken crockery, and there was a terrific battle all over the kitchen. To the rabbits underneath it sounded as if the floor would give way at each crash of falling furniture.

They crept out of their tunnel, and hung about amongst the rocks and bushes, listening anxiously.

Inside the house the racket was fearful. The rabbit babies in the oven woke up trembling; perhaps it was fortunate they were shut up inside.

Everything was upset except the kitchen table.

And everything was broken, except the mantelpiece and the kitchen fender. The crockery was smashed to atoms.

The chairs were broken, and the window, and the clock fell with a crash, and there were handfuls of Mr. Tod's sandy whiskers.

The vases fell off the mantelpiece, the canisters fell off the shelf; the kettle fell off the hob. Tommy Brock put his foot in a jar of raspberry jam.

And the boiling water out of the kettle fell upon the tail of Mr. Tod.

When the kettle fell, Tommy Brock, who was still grinning, happened to be uppermost; and he rolled Mr. Tod over and over like a log, out at the door.

Then the snarling and worrying went on outside; and they rolled over the bank, and down hill, bumping over the rocks. There will never be any love lost between Tommy Brock and Mr. Tod.

As soon as the coast was clear, Peter Rabbit and Benjamin Bunny came out of the bushes—

'Now for it! Run in, Cousin Benjamin! Run in and get them! while I watch at the door.'

But Benjamin was frightened—

'Oh; oh! they are coming back!'

'No they are not.'

'Yes they are!'

'What dreadful bad language! I think they have fallen down the stone quarry.'

Still Benjamin hesitated, and Peter kept pushing him—

'Be quick, it's all right. Shut the oven door, Cousin Benjamin, so that he won't miss them.'

Decidedly there were lively doings in Mr. Tod's kitchen!

At home in the rabbit hole, things had not been quite comfortable.

After quarrelling at supper, Flopsy and old Mr. Bouncer had passed a sleepless night, and quarrelled again at breakfast. Old Mr. Bouncer could no longer deny that he had invited company into the rabbit hole; but he refused to reply to the questions and reproaches of Flopsy. The day passed heavily.

Old Mr. Bouncer, very sulky, was huddled up in a corner, barricaded with a chair. Flopsy had taken away his pipe and hidden the tobacco. She had been having a complete turn out and spring-cleaning, to relieve her feelings. She had just finished. Old Mr. Bouncer, behind his chair, was wondering anxiously what she would do next.

In Mr. Tod's kitchen, amongst the wreckage, Benjamin Bunny picked his way to the oven nervously, through a thick cloud of dust. He opened the oven door, felt inside, and found something warm and wriggling. He lifted it out carefully, and rejoined Peter Rabbit.

'I've got them! Can we get away? Shall we hide, Cousin Peter?'

Peter pricked his ears; distant sounds of fighting still echoed in the wood.

Five minutes afterwards two breathless rabbits came scuttering away down Bull Banks, half carrying half dragging a sack between them, bumpetty bump over the grass. They reached home safely and burst into the rabbit hole.

Great was old Mr. Bouncer's relief and Flopsy's joy when Peter and Benjamin arrived in triumph with the young family. The rabbit-babies were rather tumbled and very hungry; they were fed and put to bed. They soon recovered.

A long new pipe and a fresh supply of rabbit to-bacco was presented to Mr.

Bouncer. He was rather upon his dignity; but he accepted.

Old Mr. Bouncer was forgiven, and they all had dinner. Then Peter and Benjamin told their story—but they had not waited long enough to be able to tell the end of the battle between Tommy Brock and Mr. Tod.

THE TALE OF
TOM KITTEN

ONCE upon a time there were three little kittens, and their names were Mittens, Tom Kitten, and Moppet.

They had dear little fur coats of their own; and they tumbled about the doorstep and played in the dust.

But one day their mother—Mrs. Tabitha Twitchit—expected friends to tea ; so she fetched the kittens indoors, to wash and dress them, before the fine company arrived.

First she scrubbed their faces (this one is Moppet).

Then she brushed their fur, (this one is Mittens).

Then she combed their tails and whiskers (this is Tom Kitten).

Tom was very naughty, and he scratched.

Mrs. Tabitha dressed Moppet and Mittens in clean pinafores and tuckers; and then she took all sorts of elegant uncomfortable clothes out of a chest of drawers, in order to dress up her son Thomas.

Tom Kitten was very fat, and he had grown; several buttons burst off. His mother sewed them on again.

When the three kittens were ready, Mrs. Tabitha unwisely turned them out into the garden, to be out of the way while she made hot buttered toast.

'Now keep your frocks clean, children! You must walk on your hind legs. Keep away from the dirty ash-pit, and from Sally Henny Penny, and from the pig-stye and the Puddle-Ducks.'

Moppet and Mittens walked down the garden path unsteadily. Presently they trod upon their pinafores and fell on their noses.

When they stood up there were several green smears!

'Let us climb up the rockery, and sit on the garden wall,' said Moppet.

They turned their pinafores back to front, and went up with a skip and a jump; Moppet's white tucker fell down into the road.

Tom Kitten was quite unable to jump when walking upon his hind legs in trousers. He came up the rockery by degrees, breaking the ferns, and shedding buttons right and left.

He was all in pieces when he reached the top of the wall.

Moppet and Mittens tried to pull him together; his hat fell off, and the rest of his buttons burst.

While they were in difficulties, there was a pit pat paddle pat! and the three Puddle-Ducks came along the hard high road, marching one behind the other and doing the goose step— pit pat paddle pat! pit pat waddle pat!

They stopped and stood in a row, and stared up at the kittens. They had very small eyes and looked surprised.

Then the two duck-birds, Rebeccah and Jemima Puddle-Duck, picked up the hat and tucker and put them on.

Mittens laughed so that she fell off the wall. Moppet and Tom descended after her; the pinafores and all the rest of Tom's clothes came off on the way down.

'Come! Mr. Drake Puddle-Duck,' said Moppet—'Come and help us to dress him! Come and button up Tom!'
Mr. Drake Puddle-Duck advanced in a slow sideways manner, and picked up the various articles.

But he put them on *himself!* They fitted him even worse than Tom Kitten.

'It's a very fine morning!' said Mr. Drake Puddle-Duck.

And he and Jemima and Rebeccah Puddle-Duck set off up the road, keeping step—pit pat, paddle pat! pit pat, waddle pat!

Then Tabitha Twitchit came down the garden and found her kittens on the wall with no clothes on.

She pulled them off the wall, smacked them, and took them back to the house.

'My friends will arrive in a minute, and you are not fit to be seen; I am affronted,' said Mrs. Tabitha Twitchit.

She sent them upstairs; and I am sorry to say she told her friends that they were in bed with the measles; which was not true.

Quite the contrary; they were not in bed: *not* in the least.

Somehow there were very extraordinary noises overhead, which disturbed the dignity and repose of the tea party.

And I think that some day I shall have to make another, larger, book, to tell you more about Tom Kitten!

As for the Puddle-Ducks—they went into a pond.

The clothes all came off directly, because there were no buttons.

And Mr. Drake Puddle-Duck, and Jemima and Rebeccah, have been looking for them ever since.

THE TALE OF
SAMUEL WHISKERS
OR
THE ROLY-POLY PUDDING

ONCE upon a time there was an old cat, called Mrs. Tabitha Twitchit, who was an anxious parent. She used to lose her kittens continually, and whenever they were lost they were always in mischief!

On baking day she determined to shut them up in a cupboard.

She caught Moppet and Mittens, but she could not find Tom.

Mrs. Tabitha went up and down all over the house, mewing for Tom Kitten. She looked in the pantry under the staircase, and she searched the best spare bedroom that was all covered up with dust sheets. She went right upstairs and looked into the attics, but she could not find him anywhere.

It was an old, old house, full of cupboards and passages. Some of the walls were four feet thick, and there used to be queer noises inside them, as if there might be a little secret staircase. Certainly there were odd little jagged doorways in the wainscot, and things disappeared at night—especially cheese and bacon.

Mrs. Tabitha became more and more distracted, and mewed dreadfully.

While their mother was searching the house, Moppet and Mittens had got into mischief.

The cupboard door was not locked, so they pushed it open and came out.

They went straight to the dough which was set to rise in a pan before the fire.

They patted it with their little soft paws—'Shall we make dear little muffins?' said Mittens to Moppet.

But just at that moment somebody knocked at the front door, and Moppet jumped into the flour barrel in a fright.

Mittens ran away to the dairy, and hid in an empty jar on the stone shelf where the milk pans stand.

The visitor was a neighbour, Mrs. Ribby; she had called to borrow some yeast.

Mrs. Tabitha came downstairs mewing dreadfully—'Come in, Cousin Ribby, come in, and sit ye down! I'm in sad trouble, Cousin Ribby,' said Tabitha, shedding tears. 'I've lost my dear son Thomas; I'm afraid the rats have got him.' She wiped her eyes with her apron.

'He's a bad kitten, Cousin Tabitha; he made a cat's cradle of my best bonnet last time I came to tea. Where have you looked for him?'

'All over the house! The rats are too many for me. What a thing it is to have an unruly family!' said Mrs. Tabitha Twitchit.

'I'm not afraid of rats; I will help you to find him; and whip him too! What is all that soot in the fender?'

'The chimney wants sweeping—Oh, dear me, Cousin Ribby—now Moppet and Mittens are gone!'

'They have both got out of the cupboard!'

Ribby and Tabitha set to work to search the house thoroughly again. They poked under the beds with Ribby's umbrella, and they rummaged in cupboards. They even fetched a candle, and looked inside a clothes chest in one of the attics. They could not find anything, but once they heard a door bang and somebody scuttered downstairs.

'Yes, it is infested with rats,' said Tabitha tearfully. 'I caught seven young ones out of one hole in the back kitchen, and we had them for dinner last Saturday. And once I saw the old father rat—an enormous old rat, Cousin Ribby. I was just going to jump upon him, when he showed his yellow teeth at me and whisked down the hole.'

'The rats get upon my nerves, Cousin Ribby,' said Tabitha.

Ribby and Tabitha searched and searched. They both heard a curious roly-poly noise under the attic floor. But there was nothing to be seen.

They returned to the kitchen. 'Here's one of your kittens at least,' said Ribby, dragging Moppet out of the flour barrel.

They shook the flour off her and set her down on the kitchen floor. She seemed to be in a terrible fright.

'Oh! Mother, Mother,' said Moppet, 'there's been an old woman rat in the kitchen, and she's stolen some of the dough!'

The two cats ran to look at the dough pan. Sure enough there were marks of little scratching fingers, and a lump of dough was gone!

'Which way did she go, Moppet?'

But Moppet had been too much frightened to peep out of the barrel again.

Ribby and Tabitha took her with them to keep her safely in sight, while they went on with their search.

They went into the dairy.

The first thing they found was Mittens, hiding in an empty jar.

They tipped up the jar, and she scrambled out.

'Oh, Mother, Mother!' said Mittens—

'Oh! Mother, Mother, there has been an old man rat in the dairy—a dreadful 'normous big rat, mother; and he's stolen a pat of butter and the rolling-pin.'

Ribby and Tabitha looked at one another.

'A rolling-pin and butter! Oh, my poor son Thomas!' exclaimed Tabitha, wringing her paws.

'A rolling-pin?' said Ribby. 'Did we not hear a roly-poly noise in the attic when we were looking into that chest?'

Ribby and Tabitha rushed upstairs again. Sure enough the roly-poly noise was still going on quite distinctly under the attic floor.

'This is serious, Cousin Tabitha,' said Ribby. 'We must send for John Joiner at once, with a saw.'

. . . . . .

Now this is what had been happening to Tom Kitten, and it shows how very unwise it is to go up a chimney in a very old house, where a person does not know his way, and where there are enormous rats.

Tom Kitten did not want to be shut up in a cupboard. When he saw that his mother was going to bake, he determined to hide.

He looked about for a nice convenient place, and he fixed upon the chimney.

The fire had only just been lighted, and it was not hot; but there was a white choky smoke from the green sticks. Tom Kitten got upon the fender and looked up. It was a big old-fashioned fire-place.

The chimney itself was wide enough inside for a man to stand up and walk about. So there was plenty of room for a little Tom Cat.

He jumped right up into the fire-place, balancing himself upon the iron bar where the kettle hangs.

Tom Kitten took another big jump off the bar, and landed on a ledge high up inside the chimney, knocking down some soot into the fender.

Tom Kitten coughed and choked with the smoke; and he could hear the sticks beginning to crackle and burn in the fire-place down below. He made up his mind to climb right to the top, and get out on the slates, and try to catch spar-rows.

'I cannot go back. If I slipped I might fall in the fire and singe my beautiful tail and my little blue jacket.'

The chimney was a very big old-fashioned one. It was built in the days when people burnt logs of wood upon the hearth.

The chimney stack stood up above the roof like a little stone tower, and the daylight shone down from the top under the slanting slates that kept out the rain.

Tom Kitten was getting very frightened! He climbed up, and up, and up.

Then he waded sideways through inches of soot. He was like a little sweep himself.

It was most confusing in the dark. One flue seemed to lead into another.

There was less smoke, but Tom Kitten felt quite lost.

He scrambled up and up; but before he reached the chimney top he came to a place where somebody had loosened a stone in the wall. There were some mutton bones lying about—

'This seems funny,' said Tom Kitten. 'Who has been gnawing bones up here in the chimney? I wish I had never come! And what a funny smell? It is something like mouse; only dreadfully strong. It makes me sneeze,' said Tom Kitten.

He squeezed his way through the hole in the wall, and dragged himself along a most uncomfortably tight passage where there was scarcely any light.

He groped his way carefully for several yards; he was at the back of the skirting-board in the attic, where there is a little mark * in the picture.

All at once he fell head over heels in the dark, down a hole, and landed on a heap of very dirty rags.

When Tom Kitten picked himself up and looked about him—he found himself in a place that he had never seen before, although he had lived all his life in the house.

It was a very small stuffy fusty room, with boards, and rafters, and cobwebs, and lath and plaster.

Opposite to him—as far away as he could sit—was an enormous rat.

'What do you mean by tumbling into my bed all covered with smuts?' said the rat, chattering his teeth.

'Please sir, the chimney wants sweeping,' said poor Tom Kitten.

'Anna Maria! Anna Maria!' squeaked the rat. There was a pattering noise and an old woman rat poked her head round a rafter.

All in a minute she rushed upon Tom Kitten, and before he knew what was happening—

His coat was pulled off, and he was rolled up in a bundle, and tied with string in very hard knots.

Anna Maria did the tying. The old rat watched her and took snuff. When she had finished, they both sat staring at him with their mouths open.

'Anna Maria,' said the old man rat (whose name was Samuel Whiskers),—'Anna Maria, make me a kitten dumpling roly-poly pudding for my dinner.'

'It requires dough and a pat of butter, and a rolling-pin,' said Anna Maria, considering Tom Kitten with her head on one side.

'No,' said Samuel Whiskers, 'make it properly, Anna Maria, with breadcrumbs.'

'Nonsense! Butter and dough,' replied Anna Maria.

The two rats consulted together for a few minutes and then went away.

Samuel Whiskers got through a hole in the wainscot, and went boldly down the front staircase to the dairy to get the butter. He did not meet anybody.

He made a second journey for the rolling-pin. He pushed it in front of him with his paws, like a brewer's man trundling a barrel.

He could hear Ribby and Tabitha talking, but they were busy lighting the candle to look into the chest.

They did not see him.

Anna Maria went down by way of the skirting-board and a window shutter to the kitchen to steal the dough.

She borrowed a small saucer, and scooped up the dough with her paws.

She did not observe Moppet.

While Tom Kitten was left alone under the floor of the attic, he wriggled about and tried to mew for help.

But his mouth was full of soot and cobwebs, and he was tied up in such very tight knots, he could not make anybody hear him.

Except a spider, which came out of a crack in the ceiling and examined the knots critically, from a safe distance.

It was a judge of knots because it had a habit of tying up unfortunate blue-bottles. It did not offer to assist him.

Tom Kitten wriggled and squirmed until he was quite exhausted.

Presently the rats came back and set to work to make him into a dumpling. First they smeared him with butter, and then they rolled him in the dough.

'Will not the string be very indigestible, Anna Maria?' inquired Samuel Whiskers.

Anna Maria said she thought that it was of no consequence; but she wished that Tom Kitten would hold his head still, as it disarranged the pastry. She laid hold of his ears.

Tom Kitten bit and spat, and mewed and wriggled; and the rolling-pin went roly-poly, roly; roly, poly, roly. The rats each held an end.

'His tail is sticking out! You did not fetch enough dough, Anna Maria.'

'I fetched as much as I could carry,' replied Anna Maria.

'I do not think'—said Samuel Whiskers, pausing to take a look at Tom Kitten—'I do *not* think it will be a good pudding. It smells sooty.'

Anna Maria was about to argue the point, when all at once there began to be other sounds up above—the rasping noise of a saw; and the noise of a little dog, scratching and yelping!

The rats dropped the rolling-pin, and listened attentively.

'We are discovered and interrupted, Anna Maria; let us collect our property—and other people's,—and depart at once.'

'Come away at once and help me to tie up some mutton bones in a counterpane,' said Anna Maria. 'I have got half a smoked ham hidden in the chimney.'

So it happened that by the time John Joiner had got the plank up—there was nobody under the floor except the rolling-pin and Tom Kitten in a very dirty dumpling!

But there was a strong smell of rats; and John Joiner spent the rest of the morning sniffing and whining, and wagging his tail, and going round and round with his head in the hole like a gimlet.

Then he nailed the plank down again and put his tools in his bag, and came downstairs.

The cat family had quite recovered. They invited him to stay to dinner.

The dumpling had been peeled off Tom Kitten, and made separately into a bag pudding, with currants in it to hide the smuts.

They had been obliged to put Tom Kitten into a hot bath to get the butter off.

John Joiner smelt the pudding; but he regretted that he had not time to stay to dinner, because he had just finished making a wheel-barrow for Miss Potter, and she had ordered two hen-coops.

And when I was going to the post late in the afternoon—
I looked up the lane from the corner, and I saw Mr. Samuel
Whiskers and his wife on the run, with big bundles on a
little wheel-barrow, which looked very like mine.

They were just turning in at the gate to the barn of
Farmer Potatoes.

Samuel Whiskers was puffing and out of breath. Anna
Maria was still arguing in shrill tones.

She seemed to know her
way, and she seemed to
have a quantity of luggage.

I am sure *I* never gave
her leave to borrow my
wheel-barrow!

They went into the barn,
and hauled their parcels
with a bit of string to the
top of the hay mow.

After that, there were no more rats for a long time at Tabitha Twitchit's.

As for Farmer Potatoes, he has been driven nearly distracted. There are rats, and rats, and rats in his barn! They eat up the chicken food, and steal the oats and bran, and make holes in the meal bags.

And they are all descended from Mr. and Mrs. Samuel Whiskers—children and grand-children and great great grand-children.

There is no end to them!

Moppet and Mittens have grown up into very good rat-catchers.

They go out rat-catching in the village, and they find plenty of employment. They charge so much a dozen, and earn their living very comfortably.

They hang up the rats' tails in a row on the barn door, to show how many they have caught—dozens and dozens of them.

But Tom Kitten has always been afraid of a rat; he never durst face anything that is bigger than—

A Mouse.

THE TALE OF
GINGER AND PICKLES

ONCE upon a time there was a village shop. The name over the window was 'Ginger and Pickles.'

It was a little small shop just the right size for Dolls—Lucinda and Jane Doll-cook always bought their groceries at Ginger and Pickles.

The counter inside was a convenient height for rabbits. Ginger and Pickles sold red spotty pocket-handkerchiefs at a penny three farthings.

They also sold sugar, and snuff and galoshes.

In fact, although it was such a small shop it sold nearly everything—except a few things that you want in a hurry—like bootlaces, hair-pins and mutton chops.

Ginger and Pickles were the people who kept the shop. Ginger was a yellow tom-cat, and Pickles was a terrier.

The rabbits were always a little bit afraid of Pickles.

The shop was also patronized by mice—only the mice were rather afraid of Ginger.

Ginger usually requested Pickles to serve them, because he said it made his mouth water.

'I cannot bear,' said he, 'to see them going out at the door carrying their little parcels.'

'I have the same feeling about rats,' replied Pickles, 'but it would never do to eat our own customers; they would leave us and go to Tabitha Twitchit's.'

'On the contrary, they would go nowhere,' replied Ginger gloomily.

(Tabitha Twitchit kept the only other shop in the village. She did not give credit.)

Ginger and Pickles gave unlimited credit.

Now the meaning of 'credit' is this—when a customer buys a bar of soap, instead of the customer pulling out a purse and paying for it—she says she will pay another time.

And Pickles makes a low bow and says, 'With pleasure, madam,' and it is written down in a book.

The customers come again and again, and buy quantities, in spite of being afraid of Ginger and Pickles.

But there is no money in what is called the 'till.'

The customers came in crowds every day and bought quantities, especially the toffee customers. But there was always no money; they never paid for as much as a pennyworth of peppermints.

But the sales were enormous, ten times as large as Tabitha Twitchit's.

As there was always no money, Ginger and Pickles were obliged to eat their own goods.

Pickles ate biscuits and Ginger ate a dried haddock.

They ate them by candle-light after the shop was closed.

When it came to Jan. 1st there was still no money, and Pickles was unable to buy a dog licence.

' It is very unpleasant, I am afraid of the police,' said Pickles.

'It is your own fault for being a terrier; *I* do not require a licence, and neither does Kep, the Collie dog.'

'It is very uncomfortable, I am afraid I shall be summoned. I have tried in vain to get a licence upon credit at the Post Office;' said Pickles. 'The place is full of policemen. I met one as I was coming home.'

'Let us send in the bill again to Samuel Whiskers, Ginger, he owes 22/9 for bacon.'

'I do not believe that he intends to pay at all,' replied Ginger.

'And I feel sure that Anna Maria pockets things——Where are all the cream crackers?'

'You have eaten them yourself,' replied Ginger.

Ginger and Pickles retired into the back parlour.

They did accounts. They added up sums and sums, and sums.

'Samuel Whiskers has run up a bill as long as his tail; he has had an ounce and three-quarters of snuff since October.'

'What is seven pounds of butter at 1/3, and a stick of sealing wax and four matches?'

'Send in all the bills again to everybody "with comp^ts,"' replied Ginger.

After a time they heard a noise in the shop, as if something had been pushed in at the back door. They came out of the back parlour. There was an envelope lying on the counter, and a policeman writing in a note-book!

Pickles nearly had a fit, he barked and he barked and made little rushes.

'Bite him, Pickles! bite him!' spluttered Ginger behind a sugar-barrel, 'he's only a German doll!'

The policeman went on writing in his notebook; twice he put his pencil in his mouth, and once he dipped it in the treacle.

Pickles barked till he was hoarse. But still the policeman took no notice. He had bead eyes, and his helmet was sewed on with stitches.

At length on his last little rush—Pickles found that the shop was empty. The policeman had disappeared.

But the envelope remained.

'Do you think that he has gone to fetch a real live policeman? I am afraid it is a summons,' said Pickles.

'No,' replied Ginger, who had opened the envelope, 'it is the rates and taxes, £3 19 11¾.'

'This is the last straw,' said Pickles, 'let us close the shop.'

They put up the shutters, and left. But they have not removed from the neighbourhood. In fact some people wish they had gone further.

Ginger is living in the warren. I do not know what occupation he pursues; he looks stout and comfortable.

Pickles is at present a gamekeeper.

The closing of the shop caused great inconvenience. Tabitha Twitchit immediately raised the price of everything a half-penny; and she continued to refuse to give credit.

Of course there are the tradesmen's carts—the butcher, the fishman and Timothy Baker.

But a person cannot live on 'seed wigs' and sponge-cake and butter-buns—not even when the sponge-cake is as good as Timothy's!

After a time Mr. John Dormouse and his daughter began to sell peppermints and candles.

But they did not keep 'self-fitting sixes'; and it takes five mice to carry one seven inch candle.

Besides—the candles which they sell behave very strangely in warm weather.

And Miss Dormouse refused to take back the ends when they were brought back to her with complaints.

And when Mr. John Dormouse was complained to, he stayed in bed, and would say nothing but 'very snug;' which is not the way to carry on a retail business.

So everybody was pleased when Sally Henny Penny sent out a printed poster to say that she was going to re-open the shop—'Henny's Opening Sale! Grand co-operative Jumble! Penny's penny prices! Come buy, come try, come buy!'

The poster really was most 'ticing.

There was a rush upon the opening day. The shop was crammed with customers, and there were crowds of mice upon the biscuit canisters.

Sally Henny Penny gets rather flustered when she tries to count out change, and she insists on being paid cash; but she is quite harmless.

And she has laid in a remarkable assortment of bargains.

There is something to please everybody.

THE TALE OF
THE PIE AND
THE PATTY PAN

ONCE upon a time there was a Pussy-cat called Ribby, who invited a little dog called Duchess, to tea.

'Come in good time, my dear Duchess,' said Ribby's letter, 'and we will have something so very nice. I am baking it in a pie-dish—a pie-dish with a pink rim. You never tasted anything so good! And *you* shall eat it all! *I* will eat muffins, my dear Duchess!' wrote Ribby.

Duchess read the letter and wrote an answer:—'I will come with much pleasure at a quarter past four. But it is very strange. *I* was just going to invite you to come here, to supper, my dear Ribby, to eat something *most delicious*.

'I will come very punctually, my dear Ribby,' wrote Duchess; and then at the end she added—'I hope it isn't mouse?'

And then she thought that did not look quite polite; so she scratched out 'isn't mouse' and changed it to 'I hope it will be fine,' and she gave her letter to the postman.

But she thought a great deal about Ribby's pie, and she read Ribby's letter over and over again.

'I am dreadfully afraid it *will* be mouse!' said Duchess to herself—'I really couldn't, *couldn't* eat mouse pie. And I shall have to eat it, because it is a party. And *my* pie was going to be veal and ham. A pink and white pie-dish! and so is mine; just like Ribby's dishes; they were both bought at Tabitha Twitchit's.'

Duchess went into her larder and took the pie off a shelf and looked at it.

'It is all ready to put into the oven. Such lovely pie-crust; and I put in a little tin patty-pan to hold up the crust; and I made a hole in the middle with a fork to let out the steam—Oh I do wish I could eat my own pie, instead of a pie made of mouse!'

Duchess considered and considered and read Ribby's letter again—

'A pink and white pie-dish—and *you* shall eat it *all.* "You" means me—then Ribby is not going to even taste the pie herself? A pink and white pie-dish! Ribby is sure to go out to buy the muffins.... Oh what a good idea! Why shouldn't I rush along and put my pie into Ribby's oven when Ribby isn't there?'

Duchess was quite delighted with her own cleverness!

Ribby in the meantime had received Duchess's answer, and as soon as she was sure that the little dog could come—she popped *her* pie into the oven. There were two ovens, one above the other; some other knobs and handles were only ornamental and not intended to open. Ribby put the pie into the lower oven; the door was very stiff.

'The top oven bakes too quickly,' said Ribby to herself. 'It is a pie of the most delicate and tender mouse minced up with bacon. And I have taken out all the bones; because Duchess did nearly choke herself with a fish-bone last time I gave a party. She eats a little fast—rather big mouthfuls. But a most genteel and elegant little dog; infinitely superior company to Cousin Tabitha Twitchit.'

Ribby put on some coal and swept up the hearth. Then she went out with a can to the well, for water to fill up the kettle.

Then she began to set the room in order, for it was the sitting-room as well as the kitchen. She shook the mats out at the front-door and put them straight; the hearth-rug was a rabbit-skin. She dusted the clock and the ornaments on the mantelpiece, and she polished and rubbed the tables and chairs.

Then she spread a very clean white table-cloth, and set out her best china tea-set, which she took out of a wall-cupboard near the fireplace. The tea-cups were white with a pattern of pink roses; and the dinner-plates were white and blue.

When Ribby had laid the table she took a jug and a blue and white dish, and went out down the field to the farm, to fetch milk and butter.

When she came back, she peeped into the bottom oven; the pie looked very comfortable.

Ribby put on her shawl and bonnet and went out again with a basket, to the village shop to buy a packet of tea, a pound of lump sugar, and a pot of marmalade.

And just at the same time, Duchess came out of *her* house, at the other end of the village.

Ribby met Duchess halfway down the street, also carrying a basket, covered with a cloth. They only bowed to one another; they did not speak, because they were going to have a party.

As soon as Duchess had got round the corner out of sight—she simply ran! Straight away to Ribby's house!

Ribby went into the shop and bought what she required, and came out, after a pleasant gossip with Cousin Tabitha Twitchit.

Cousin Tabitha was disdainful afterwards in conversation—

'A little *dog* indeed! Just as if there were no CATS in Sawrey! And a *pie* for afternoon tea! The very idea!' said Cousin Tabitha Twitchit.

Ribby went on to Timothy Baker's and bought the muffins. Then she went home.

There seemed to be a sort of scuffling noise in the back passage, as she was coming in at the front door.

'I trust that is not that Pie: the spoons are locked up, however,' said Ribby.

But there was nobody there. Ribby opened the bottom oven door with some difficulty, and turned the pie. There began to be a pleasing smell of baked mouse!

Duchess in the meantime, had slipped out at the back door.

'It is a very odd thing that Ribby's pie was *not* in the oven when I put mine in! And I can't find it anywhere; I have looked all over the house. I put *my* pie into a nice hot oven at the top. I could not turn any of the other handles; I think that they are all shams,' said Duchess, 'but I wish I could have removed the pie made of mouse! I cannot think what she has done with it? I heard Ribby coming and I had to run out by the back door!'

Duchess went home and brushed her beautiful black coat; and then she picked a bunch of flowers in her garden as a present for Ribby; and passed the time until the clock struck four.

Ribby—having assured herself by careful search that there was really no one hiding in the cupboard or in the larder—went upstairs to change her dress.

She put on a lilac silk gown, for the party, and an embroidered muslin apron and tippet.

'It is very strange,' said Ribby, 'I did not *think* I left that drawer pulled out; has somebody been trying on my mittens?'

She came downstairs again and made the tea, and put the teapot on the hob. She peeped again into the *bottom* oven, the pie had become a lovely brown, and it was steaming hot.

She sat down before the fire to wait for the little dog. 'I am glad I used the *bottom* oven,' said Ribby, 'the top one would certainly have been very much too hot. I wonder why that cupboard door was open? Can there really have been someone in the house?'

Very punctually at four o'clock, Duchess started to go to the party. She ran so fast through the village that she was too early, and she had to wait a little while in the lane that leads down to Ribby's house.

'I wonder if Ribby has taken *my* pie out of the oven yet?' said Duchess, 'and whatever can have become of the other pie made of mouse?'

At a quarter past four to the minute, there came a most genteel little tap-tappity. 'Is Mrs. Ribston at home?' inquired Duchess in the porch.

'Come in! and how do you do, my dear Duchess?' cried Ribby. 'I hope I see you well?'

'Quite well, I thank you, and how do *you* do, my dear Ribby?' said Duchess. 'I've brought you some flowers; what a delicious smell of pie!'

'Oh, what lovely flowers! Yes, it is mouse and bacon!'

'Do not talk about food, my dear Ribby,' said Duchess; 'what a lovely white tea-cloth!.... Is it done to a turn? Is it still in the oven?'

'I think it wants another five minutes,' said Ribby. 'Just a shade longer; I will pour out the tea, while we wait. Do you take sugar, my dear Duchess?'

'Oh yes, please! my dear Ribby; and may I have a lump upon my nose?'

'With pleasure, my dear Duchess; how beautifully you beg! Oh, how sweetly pretty!'

Duchess sat up with the sugar on her nose and sniffed—

'How good that pie smells! I do love veal and ham—I mean to say mouse and bacon——'

She dropped the sugar in confusion, and had to go hunting under the tea-table, so did not see which oven Ribby opened in order to get out the pie.

Ribby set the pie upon the table; there was a very savoury smell.

Duchess came out from under the table-cloth munching sugar, and sat up on a chair.

'I will first cut the pie for you; I am going to have muffin and marmalade,' said Ribby.

'Do you really prefer muffin? Mind the patty-pan!'

'I beg your pardon?' said Ribby.

'May I pass you the marmalade?' said Duchess hurriedly.

The pie proved extremely toothsome, and the muffins light and hot. They disappeared rapidly, especially the pie!

'I think'—(thought the Duchess to herself)—'I *think* it would be wiser if I helped myself to pie; though Ribby did not seem to notice anything when she was cutting it. What very small fine pieces it has cooked into! I did not remember that I had minced it up so fine; I suppose this is a quicker oven than my own.'

'How fast Duchess is eating!' thought Ribby to herself, as she buttered her fifth muffin.

The pie-dish was emptying rapidly! Duchess had had four helps already, and was fumbling with the spoon.

'A little more bacon, my dear Duchess?' said Ribby.

'Thank you, my dear Ribby; I was only feeling for the patty-pan.'

'The patty-pan? my dear Duchess?'

'The patty-pan that held up the pie-crust,' said Duchess, blushing under her black coat.

'Oh, I didn't put one in, my dear Duchess,' said Ribby; 'I don't think that it is necessary in pies made of mouse.'

Duchess fumbled with the spoon—'I can't find it!' she said anxiously.

'There isn't a patty-pan,' said Ribby, looking perplexed.

'Yes, indeed, my dear Ribby; where can it have gone to?' said Duchess.

'There most certainly is not one, my dear Duchess. I disapprove of tin articles in puddings and pies. It is most undesirable—(especially when people swallow in lumps!)' she added in a lower voice.

Duchess looked very much alarmed, and continued to scoop the inside of the pie-dish.

'My Great-aunt Squintina (grandmother of Cousin Tabitha Twitchit)—died of a thimble in a Christmas plum-pudding. *I* never put any article of metal in *my* puddings or pies.'

Duchess looked aghast, and tilted up the pie-dish.

'I have only four patty-pans, and they are all in the cupboard.'

Duchess set up a howl.

'I shall die! I shall die! I have swallowed a patty-pan! Oh, my dear Ribby, I do feel so ill!'

'It is impossible, my dear Duchess; there was not a patty-pan.'

Duchess moaned and whined and rocked herself about.

'Oh I feel so dreadful, I have swallowed a patty-pan!'

'There was *nothing* in the pie,' said Ribby severely.

'Yes there *was*, my dear Ribby, I am sure I have swallowed it!'

'Let me prop you up with a pillow, my dear Duchess; where do you think you feel it?'

'Oh I do feel so ill *all over* me, my dear Ribby; I have swallowed a large tin patty-pan with a sharp scalloped edge!'

'Shall I run for the doctor? I will just lock up the spoons!'

'Oh yes, yes! fetch Dr. Maggotty, my dear Ribby: he is a Pie himself, he will certainly understand.'

Ribby settled Duchess in an armchair before the fire, and went out and hurried to the village to look for the doctor.

She found him at the smithy.

He was occupied in putting rusty nails into a bottle of ink, which he had obtained at the post office.

'Gammon? ha! HA!' said he, with his head on one side.

Ribby explained that her guest had swallowed a patty-pan.

'Spinach? ha! HA!' said he, and accompanied her with alacrity.

He hopped so fast that Ribby had to run. It was most conspicuous. All the village could see that Ribby was fetching the doctor.

'I *knew* they would over-eat themselves!' said Cousin Tabitha Twitchit.

But while Ribby had been hunting for the doctor—a curious thing had happened to Duchess, who had been left by herself, sitting before the fire, sighing and groaning and feeling very unhappy.

'How *could* I have swallowed it! such a large thing as a patty-pan!'

She got up and went to the table, and felt inside the pie-dish again with a spoon.

'No; there is no patty-pan, and I put one in; and nobody has eaten pie except me, so I must have swallowed it!'

She sat down again, and stared mournfully at the grate. The fire crackled and danced, and something sizz-z-zled!

Duchess started! She opened the door of the *top* oven;—out came a rich steamy flavour of veal and ham, and there stood a fine brown pie,—and through a hole in the top of the pie-crust there was a glimpse of a little tin patty-pan!

Duchess drew a long breath—

'Then I must have been eating MOUSE!... No wonder I feel ill .... But perhaps I should feel worse if I had really swallowed a patty-pan!' Duchess reflected—'What a very awkward thing to have to explain to Ribby! I think I will put *my* pie in the back-yard and say nothing about it. When I go home, I will run round and take it away.'

She put it outside the back-door, and sat down again by the fire, and shut her eyes; when Ribby arrived with the doctor, she seemed fast asleep.

'Gammon, ha, HA?' said the doctor.

'I am feeling very much better,' said Duchess, waking up with a jump.

'I am truly glad to hear it! He has brought you a pill, my dear Duchess!'

'I think I should feel *quite* well if he only felt my pulse,' said Duchess, backing away from the magpie, who sidled up with something in his beak.

'It is only a bread pill, you had much better take it; drink a little milk, my dear Duchess!'

'Gammon? Gammon?' said the doctor, while Duchess coughed and choked.

'Don't say that again!' said Ribby, losing her temper— 'Here, take this bread and jam, and get out into the yard!'

'Gammon and Spinach! ha ha HA!' shouted Dr. Maggotty triumphantly outside the back door.

'I am feeling very much better my dear Ribby,' said Duchess. 'Do you not think that I had better go home before it gets dark?'

'Perhaps it might be wise, my dear Duchess. I will lend you a nice warm shawl, and you shall take my arm.'

'I would not trouble you for worlds; I feel wonderfully better. One pill of Dr. Maggotty——'

'Indeed it is most admirable, if it has cured you of a patty-pan! I will call directly after breakfast to ask how you have slept.'

Ribby and Duchess said goodbye affectionately, and Duchess started home. Half-way up the lane she stopped and looked back; Ribby had gone in and shut her door. Duchess slipped through the fence, and ran round to the back of Ribby's house, and peeped into the yard.

Upon the roof of the pig-stye sat Dr. Maggotty and three jackdaws. The jackdaws were eating pie-crust, and the magpie was drinking gravy out of a patty-pan.

'Gammon, ha, HA!' he shouted when he saw Duchess's little black nose peeping round the corner.

Duchess ran home feeling uncommonly silly!

When Ribby came out for a pailful of water to wash up the tea-things, she found a pink and white pie-dish lying smashed in the middle of the yard. The patty-pan was under the pump, where Dr. Maggotty had considerately left it.

Ribby stared with amazement—'Did you ever see the like! so there really *was* a patty-pan? .... But *my* patty-pans are all in the kitchen cupboard. Well I never did! .... Next time I want to give a party—I will invite Cousin Tabitha Twitchit!'

THE STORY OF
MISS MOPPET

THIS is a Pussy called Miss Moppet, she thinks she has heard a mouse!

This is the Mouse peeping out behind the cupboard, and making fun of Miss Moppet. He is not afraid of a kitten.

This is Miss Moppet jumping just too late; she misses the Mouse and hits her own head.

She thinks it is a very hard cupboard!

The Mouse watches Miss Moppet from the top of the cupboard.

Miss Moppet ties up her head in a duster, and sits before the fire.

The Mouse thinks she is looking very ill. He comes sliding down the bell-pull.

Miss Moppet looks worse and worse. The Mouse comes a little nearer.

Miss Moppet holds her poor head in her paws, and looks at him through a hole in the duster. The Mouse comes *very* close.

And then all of a sudden—Miss Moppet jumps upon the Mouse!

And because the Mouse has teased Miss Moppet— Miss Moppet thinks she will tease the Mouse; which is not at all nice of Miss Moppet.

She ties him up in the duster, and tosses it about like a ball.

But she forgot about that hole in the duster; and when she untied it—there was no Mouse!

He has wriggled out and run away; and he is dancing a jig on the top of the cupboard!

THE TALE OF
JEMIMA PUDDLE-DUCK

A Farmyard Tale
for
Ralph and Betsy

WHAT a funny sight it is to see a brood of ducklings with a hen!

—Listen to the story of Jemima Puddle-duck, who was annoyed because the farmer's wife would not let her hatch her own eggs.

Her sister-in-law, Mrs. Rebeccah Puddle-duck, was perfectly willing to leave the hatching to some one else— 'I have not the patience to sit on a nest for twenty-eight days; and no more have you, Jemima. You would let them go cold; you know you would!'

'I wish to hatch my own eggs; I will hatch them all by myself,' quacked Jemima Puddle-duck.

She tried to hide her eggs; but they were always found and carried off.

Jemima Puddle-duck became quite desperate. She determined to make a nest right away from the farm.

She set off on a fine spring afternoon along the cart-road that leads over the hill.

She was wearing a shawl and a poke bonnet.

When she reached the top of the hill, she saw a wood in the distance.

She thought that it looked a safe quiet spot.

Jemima Puddle-duck was not much in the habit of flying. She ran downhill a few yards flapping her shawl, and then she jumped off into the air.

She flew beautifully when she had got a good start.

She skimmed along over the tree-tops until she saw an open place in the middle of the wood, where the trees and brushwood had been cleared.

Jemima alighted rather heavily, and began to waddle about in search of a convenient dry nesting-place. She rather fancied a tree-stump amongst some tall fox-gloves.

But—seated upon the stump, she was startled to find an elegantly dressed gentleman reading a newspaper.

He had black prick ears and sandy coloured whiskers.

'Quack?' said Jemima Puddle-duck, with her head and her bonnet on one side—'Quack?'

The gentleman raised his eyes above his newspaper and looked curiously at Jemima—

'Madam, have you lost your way?' said he. He had a long bushy tail which he was sitting upon, as the stump was somewhat damp.

Jemima thought him mighty civil and handsome. She explained that she had not lost her way, but that she was trying to find a convenient dry nesting-place.

'Ah! is that so? indeed!' said the gentleman with sandy whiskers, looking curiously at Jemima. He folded up the newspaper, and put it in his coat-tail pocket.

Jemima complained of the superfluous hen.

'Indeed! how interesting! I wish I could meet with that fowl. I would teach it to mind its own business!

'But as to a nest—there is no difficulty: I have a sackful of feathers in my wood-shed. No, my dear madam, you will be in nobody's way. You may sit there as long as you like,' said the bushy long-tailed gentleman.

He led the way to a very retired, dismal-looking house amongst the fox-gloves.

It was built of faggots and turf, and there were two broken pails, one on top of another, by way of a chimney.

'This is my summer residence; you would not find my earth—my winter house—so convenient,' said the hospitable gentleman.

There was a tumble-down shed at the back of the house, made of old soap-boxes. The gentleman opened the door, and showed Jemima in.

The shed was almost quite full of feathers—it was almost suffocating; but it was comfortable and very soft.

Jemima Puddle-duck was rather surprised to find such a vast quantity of feathers. But it was very comfortable; and she made a nest without any trouble at all.

When she came out, the sandy whiskered gentleman was sitting on a log reading the newspaper—at least he had it spread out, but he was looking over the top of it.

He was so polite, that he seemed almost sorry to let Jemima go home for the night. He promised to take great care of her nest until she came back again next day.

He said he loved eggs and ducklings; he should be proud to see a fine nestful in his wood-shed.

Jemima Puddle-duck came every afternoon; she laid nine eggs in the nest. They were greeny white and very large. The foxy gentleman admired them immensely. He used to turn them over and count them when Jemima was not there.

At last Jemima told him that she intended to begin to sit next day—'and I will bring a bag of corn with me, so that I need never leave my nest until the eggs are hatched. They might catch cold,' said the conscientious Jemima.

'Madam, I beg you not to trouble yourself with a bag; I will provide oats. But before you commence your tedious sitting, I intend to give you a treat. Let us have a dinner-party all to ourselves!

'May I ask you to bring up some herbs from the farm-garden to make a savoury omelette? Sage and thyme, and mint and two onions, and some parsley. I will provide lard for the stuff—lard for the omelette,' said the hospitable gentleman with sandy whiskers.

Jemima Puddle-duck was a simpleton: not even the mention of sage and onions made her suspicious.

She went round the farm-garden, nibbling off snippets of all the different sorts of herbs that are used for stuffing roast duck.

And she waddled into the kitchen, and got two onions out of a basket.

The collie-dog Kep met her coming out, 'What are you doing with those onions? Where do you go every afternoon by yourself, Jemima Puddle-duck?'

Jemima was rather in awe of the collie; she told him the whole story.

The collie listened, with his wise head on one side; he grinned when she described the polite gentleman with sandy whiskers.

He asked several questions about the wood, and about the exact position of the house and shed.

Then he went out, and trotted down the village. He went to look for two fox-hound puppies who were out at walk with the butcher.

Jemima Puddle-duck went up the cart-road for the last time, on a sunny afternoon. She was rather burdened with bunches of herbs and two onions in a bag.

She flew over the wood, and alighted opposite the house of the bushy long-tailed gentleman.

He was sitting on a log; he sniffed the air, and kept glancing uneasily round the wood. When Jemima alighted he quite jumped.

'Come into the house as soon as you have looked at your eggs. Give me the herbs for the omelette. Be sharp!'

He was rather abrupt. Jemima Puddle-duck had never heard him speak like that.

She felt surprised, and uncomfortable.

While she was inside she heard pattering feet round the back of the shed. Some one with a black nose sniffed at the bottom of the door, and then locked it.

Jemima became much alarmed.

A moment afterwards there were most awful noises—barking, baying, growls and howls, squealing and groans.

And nothing more was ever seen of that foxy-whiskered gentleman.

Presently Kep opened the door of the shed, and let out Jemima Puddle-duck.

Unfortunately the puppies rushed in and gobbled up all the eggs before he could stop them.

He had a bite on his ear and both the puppies were limping.

Jemima Puddle-duck was escorted home in tears on account of those eggs.

She laid some more in June, and she was permitted to keep them herself: but only four of them hatched.

Jemima Puddle-duck said that it was because of her nerves; but she had always been a bad sitter.

THE TALE OF
MR. JEREMY FISHER

For
Stephanie
from
Cousin B.

ONCE upon a time there was a frog called Mr. Jeremy
Fisher; he lived in a little damp house amongst the
buttercups at the edge of a pond.

The water was all slippy-sloppy in the larder and in the back passage.

But Mr. Jeremy liked getting his feet wet; nobody ever scolded him, and he never caught a cold!

He was quite pleased when he looked out and saw large drops of rain, splashing in the pond—

'I will get some worms and go fishing and catch a dish of minnows for my dinner,' said Mr. Jeremy Fisher. 'If I catch more than five fish, I will invite my friends Mr. Alderman Ptolemy Tortoise and Sir Isaac Newton. The Alderman, however, eats salad.'

Mr. Jeremy put on a macintosh, and a pair of shiny goloshes; he took his rod and basket, and set off with enormous hops to the place where he kept his boat.

The boat was round and green, and very like the other lily-leaves. It was tied to a water-plant in the middle of the pond.

Mr. Jeremy took a reed pole, and pushed the boat out into open water. 'I know a good place for minnows,' said Mr. Jeremy Fisher.

Mr. Jeremy stuck his pole into the mud and fastened his boat to it.

Then he settled himself cross-legged and arranged his fishing tackle. He had the dearest little red float. His rod was a tough stalk of grass, his line was a fine long white horse-hair, and he tied a little wriggling worm at the end.

The rain trickled down his back, and for nearly an hour he stared at the float.

'This is getting tiresome, I think I should like some lunch,' said Mr. Jeremy Fisher.

He punted back again amongst the water-plants, and took some lunch out of his basket.

'I will eat a butterfly sandwich, and wait till the shower is over,' said Mr. Jeremy Fisher.

A great big water-beetle came up underneath the lily leaf and tweaked the toe of one of his goloshes.

Mr. Jeremy crossed his legs up shorter, out of reach, and went on eating his sandwich.

Once or twice something moved about with a rustle and a splash amongst the rushes at the side of the pond.

'I trust that is not a rat,' said Mr. Jeremy Fisher; 'I think I had better get away from here.'

Mr. Jeremy shoved the boat out again a little way, and dropped in the bait. There was a bite almost directly; the float gave a tremendous bobbit!

'A minnow! a minnow! I have him by the nose!' cried Mr. Jeremy Fisher, jerking up his rod.

But what a horrible surprise! Instead of a smooth fat minnow, Mr. Jeremy landed little Jack Sharp the stickleback, covered with spines!

The stickleback floundered about the boat, pricking and snapping until he was quite out of breath. Then he jumped back into the water.

And a shoal of other little fishes put their heads out, and laughed at Mr. Jeremy Fisher.

And while Mr. Jeremy sat disconsolately on the edge of his boat—sucking his sore fingers and peering down into the water—a *much* worse thing happened; a really *frightful* thing it would have been, if Mr. Jeremy had not been wearing a macintosh!

A great big enormous trout came up—ker-pflop-p-p-p! with a splash—and it seized Mr. Jeremy with a snap, 'Ow! Ow! Ow!'—and then it turned and dived down to the bottom of the pond!

But the trout was so displeased with the taste of the macintosh, that in less than half a minute it spat him out again; and the only thing it swallowed was Mr. Jeremy's goloshes.

Mr. Jeremy bounced up to the surface of the water, like a cork and the bubbles out of a soda water bottle; and he swam with all his might to the edge of the pond.

He scrambled out on the first bank he came to, and he hopped home across the meadow with his macintosh all in tatters.

'What a mercy that was not a pike!' said Mr. Jeremy Fisher. 'I have lost my rod and basket; but it does not much matter, for I am sure I should never have dared to go fishing again!'

He put some sticking plaster on his fingers, and his friends both came to dinner. He could not offer them fish, but he had something else in his larder.

Sir Isaac Newton wore his black and gold waistcoat.

And Mr. Alderman Ptolemy Tortoise brought a salad with him in a string bag.

And instead of a nice dish of minnows—they had a roasted grasshopper with lady-bird sauce; which frogs consider a beautiful treat; but *I* think it must have been nasty!

THE TALE OF
MRS. TIGGY-WINKLE

for
The Real Little Lucie
of Newlands

ONCE upon a time there was a little girl called Lucie, who lived at a farm called Little-town. She was a good little girl—only she was always losing her pocket-handkerchiefs!

One day little Lucie came into the farm-yard crying—oh, she did cry so! 'I've lost my pocket-handkin! Three handkins and a pinny! Have *you* seen them, Tabby Kitten?'

The Kitten went on washing her white paws; so Lucie asked a speckled hen—

'Sally Henny-penny, have *you* found three pocket-handkins?'

But the speckled hen ran into a barn, clucking—

'I go barefoot, barefoot, barefoot!'

And then Lucie asked Cock Robin sitting on a twig. Cock Robin looked sideways at Lucie with his bright black eye, and he flew over a stile and away.

Lucie climbed upon the stile and looked up at the hill behind Little-town—a hill that goes up—up—into the clouds as though it had no top!

And a great way up the hill-side she thought she saw some white things spread upon the grass.

Lucie scrambled up the hill as fast as her stout legs would carry her; she ran along a steep path-way—up and up—until Little-town was right away down below—she could have dropped a pebble down the chimney!

Presently she came to a spring, bubbling out from the hill-side.

Some one had stood a tin can upon a stone to catch the water—but the water was already running over, for the can was no bigger than an egg-cup! And where the sand upon the path was wet—there were foot-marks of a *very* small person.

Lucie ran on, and on.

The path ended under a big rock. The grass was short and green, and there were clothes-props cut from bracken stems, with lines of plaited rushes, and a heap of tiny clothes pins—but no pocket-handkerchiefs!

But there was something else—a door! straight into the hill; and inside it some one was singing—

'Lily-white and clean, oh!
With little frills between, oh!
  Smooth and hot—red rusty spot
Never here be seen, oh!'

Lucie, knocked—once—twice, and interrupted the song. A little frightened voice called out 'Who's that?'

Lucie opened the door: and what do you think there was inside the hill?— a nice clean kitchen with a flagged floor and wooden beams—just like any other farm kitchen. Only the ceiling was so low that Lucie's head nearly touched it; and the pots and pans were small, and so was everything there.

There was a nice hot singey smell; and at the table, with an iron in her hand stood a very stout short person staring anxiously at Lucie.

Her print gown was tucked up, and she was wearing a large apron over her striped petticoat. Her little black nose went sniffle, sniffle, snuffle, and her eyes went twinkle, twinkle; and underneath her cap—where Lucie had yellow curls—that little person had PRICKLES!

'Who are you?' said Lucie. 'Have you seen my pocket-handkins?'

The little person made a bob-curtsey—'Oh, yes, if you please'm; my name is Mrs. Tiggy-winkle; oh, yes if you please'm, I'm an excellent clear-starcher!' And she took something out of a clothes-basket, and spread it on the ironing-blanket.

'What's that thing?' said Lucie—'that's not my pocket-handkin?'

'Oh no, if you please'm; that's a little scarlet waist-coat belonging to Cock Robin!'

And she ironed it and folded it, and put it on one side.

Then she took something else off a clothes-horse—

'That isn't my pinny?' said Lucie.

'Oh no, if you please'm; that's a damask table-cloth belonging to Jenny Wren; look how it's stained with currant wine! It's very bad to wash!' said Mrs. Tiggy-winkle.

Mrs. Tiggy-winkle's nose went sniffle, sniffle, snuffle, and her eyes went twinkle, twinkle; and she fetched another hot iron from the fire.

'There's one of my pocket-handkins!' cried Lucie—'and there's my pinny!'

Mrs. Tiggy-winkle ironed it, and goffered it, and shook out the frills.

'Oh that *is* lovely!' said Lucie.

'And what are those long yellow things with fingers like gloves?'

'Oh, that's a pair of stockings belonging to Sally Henny-penny—look how she's worn the heels out with scratching in the yard! She'll very soon go barefoot!' said Mrs. Tiggy-winkle.

'Why, there's another handkersniff—but it isn't mine; it's red?'

'Oh no, if you please'm; that one belongs to old Mrs. Rabbit; and it *did* so smell of onions! I've had to wash it separately, I can't get out the smell.'

'There's another one of mine,' said Lucie.

'What are those funny little white things?'

'That's a pair of mittens belonging to Tabby Kitten; I only have to iron them; she washes them herself.'

'There's my last pocket-handkin!' said Lucie.

'And what are you dipping into the basin of starch?'

'They're little dicky shirt-fronts belonging to Tom Titmouse—most terrible particular!' said Mrs. Tiggy-winkle. 'Now I've finished my ironing; I'm going to air some clothes.'

'What are these dear soft fluffy things?' said Lucie.

'Oh those are woolly coats belonging to the little lambs at Skelghyl.'

'Will their jackets take off?' asked Lucie.

'Oh yes, if you please'm; look at the sheep-mark on the shoulder. And here's one marked for Gatesgarth, and three that come from Little-town. They're *always* marked at washing!' said Mrs. Tiggy-winkle.

And she hung up all sorts and sizes of clothes—small brown coats of mice; and one velvety black mole-skin waist-coat; and a red tail-coat with no tail belonging to Squirrel Nutkin; and a very much shrunk blue jacket belonging to Peter Rabbit; and a petticoat, not marked, that had gone lost in the washing—and at last the basket was empty!

Then Mrs. Tiggy-winkle made tea—a cup for herself and a cup for Lucie. They sat before the fire on a bench and looked sideways at one another. Mrs. Tiggy-winkle's hand, holding the tea-cup, was very very brown, and very very wrinkly with the soap-suds; and all through her gown and her cap, there were *hair-pins* sticking wrong end out; so that Lucie didn't like to sit too near her.

When they had finished tea, they tied up the clothes in bundles; and Lucie's pocket-handkerchiefs were folded up inside her clean pinny, and fastened with a silver safety-pin.

And then they made up the fire with turf, and came out and locked the door, and hid the key under the door-sill.

Then away down the hill
trotted Lucie and Mrs.
Tiggy-winkle with the bundles of clothes!

All the way down the
path little animals came out
of the fern to meet them;
the very first that they met
were Peter Rabbit and Benjamin Bunny!

And she gave them their nice clean clothes; and all the
little animals and birds were so very much obliged to dear
Mrs. Tiggy-winkle.

So that at the bottom of the hill when they came to the stile, there was nothing left to carry except Lucie's one little bundle.

Lucie scrambled up the stile with the bundle in her hand; and then she turned to say 'Good-night,' and to thank the washer-woman— But what a *very* odd thing! Mrs. Tiggy-winkle had not waited either for thanks or for the washing bill!

She was running running running up the hill—and where was her white frilled cap? and her shawl? and her gown—and her petticoat?

And *how* small she had grown—and *how* brown—and covered with Prickles!

Why! Mrs. Tiggy-winkle was nothing but a Hedgehog.

*   *   *   *   *

(Now some people say that little Lucie had been asleep upon the stile—but then how could she have found three clean pocket-handkins and a pinny, pinned with a silver safety-pin?

And besides—*I* have seen that door into the back of the hill called Cat Bells—and besides *I* am very well acquainted with dear Mrs. Tiggy-winkle!)

THE TALE OF
PIGLING BLAND

For
Cecily and Charlie

A Tale of
The Christmas Pig

ONCE upon a time there was an old pig called Aunt Pettitoes. She had eight of a family: four little girl pigs, called Cross-patch, Suck-suck, Yock-yock and Spot; and four little boy pigs, called Alexander, Pigling Bland, Chin-chin and Stumpy. Stumpy had had an accident to his tail.

The eight little pigs had very fine appetites. 'Yus, yus, yus! they eat and indeed they *do* eat!' said Aunt Pettitoes, looking at her family with pride. Suddenly there were fearful squeals; Alexander had squeezed inside the hoops of the pig trough and stuck.

Aunt Pettitoes and I dragged him out by the hind legs.

Chin-chin was already in disgrace; it was washing day, and he had eaten a piece of soap. And presently in a basket of clean clothes, we found another dirty little pig.

'Tchut, tut, tut! whichever is this?' grunted Aunt Pettitoes. Now all the pig family are pink, or pink with black spots, but this pig child was smutty black all over; when it had been popped into a tub, it proved to be Yock-yock.

I went into the garden; there I found Cross-patch and Suck-suck rooting up carrots. I whipped them myself and led them out by the ears. Cross-patch tried to bite me.

'Aunt Pettitoes, Aunt Pettitoes! you are a worthy person, but your family is not well brought up. Every one of them has been in mischief except Spot and Pigling Bland.'

'Yus, yus!' sighed Aunt Pettitoes. 'And they drink bucketfuls of milk; I shall have to get another cow! Good little Spot shall stay at home to do the housework; but the others must go. Four little boy pigs and four little girl pigs are too many altogether.' 'Yus, yus, yus,' said Aunt Pettitoes, 'there will be more to eat without them.'

So Chin-chin and Suck-suck went away in a wheel-barrow, and Stumpy, Yock-yock and Cross-patch rode away in a cart.

And the other two little boy pigs, Pigling Bland and Alexander, went to market. We brushed their coats, we curled their tails and washed their little faces, and wished them good-bye in the yard.

Aunt Pettitoes wiped her eyes with a large pocket handkerchief, then she wiped Pigling Bland's nose and shed tears ; then she wiped Alexander's nose and shed tears ; then she passed the handkerchief to Spot. Aunt Pettitoes sighed and grunted, and addressed those little pigs as follows :

'Now Pigling Bland, son Pigling Bland, you must go to market. Take your brother Alexander by the hand. Mind your Sunday clothes, and remember to blow your nose '— (Aunt Pettitoes passed round the handkerchief again)— 'beware of traps, hen roosts, bacon and eggs ; always walk upon your hind legs.' Pigling Bland, who was a sedate little pig, looked solemnly at his mother, a tear trickled down his cheek.

Aunt Pettitoes turned to the other—'Now son Alexander take the hand'—'Wee, wee, wee!' giggled Alexander—'take the hand of your brother Pigling Bland, you must go to market. Mind—' 'Wee, wee, wee!' interrupted Alexander again. 'You put me out,' said Aunt Pettitoes—'Observe sign-posts and milestones; do not gobble herring bones—' 'And remember,' said I impressively, 'if you once cross the county boundary you cannot come back. Alexander, you are not attending. Here are two licences permitting two pigs to go to market in Lancashire. Attend, Alexander. I have had no end of trouble in getting these papers from the policeman.' Pigling Bland listened gravely; Alexander was hopelessly volatile.

I pinned the papers, for safety, inside their waistcoat pockets; Aunt Pettitoes gave to each a little bundle, and eight conversation peppermints with appropriate moral sentiments in screws of paper. Then they started.

Pigling Bland and Alexander trotted along steadily for a mile; at least Pigling Bland did. Alexander made the road half as long again by skipping from side to side. He danced about and pinched his brother, singing—

'This pig went to market, this pig stayed at home,
'This pig had a bit of meat—

let's see what they have given *us* for dinner, Pigling?'

Pigling Bland and Alexander sat down and untied their bundles. Alexander gobbled up his dinner in no time; he had already eaten all his own peppermints. 'Give me one of yours, please, Pigling.' 'But I wish to preserve them for emergencies,' said Pigling Bland doubtfully. Alexander went into squeals of laughter. Then he pricked Pigling with the pin that had fastened his pig paper; and when Pigling slapped him he dropped the pin, and tried to take Pigling's pin, and the papers got mixed up. Pigling Bland reproved Alexander.

But presently they made it up again, and trotted away together, singing—

'Tom, Tom, the piper's son, stole a pig
    and away he ran!
'But all the tune that he could play,
    was "Over the hills and far away!"'

'What's that, young sirs? Stole a pig? Where are your licences?' said the policeman. They had nearly run against him round a corner. Pigling Bland pulled out his paper; Alexander, after fumbling, handed over something scrumply—

'To 2½ oz. conversation sweeties at three far-things'—'What's this? This ain't a licence.' Alexander's nose lengthened visibly, he had lost it. 'I had one, indeed I had, Mr. Police-man!'

'It's not likely they let you start without. I am passing the farm. You may walk with me.' 'Can I come back too?'

inquired Pigling Bland. 'I see no reason, young sir; your paper is all right.' Pigling Bland did not like going on alone, and it was beginning to rain. But it is unwise to argue with the police; he gave his brother a peppermint, and watched him out of sight.

To conclude the adventures of Alexander—the policeman sauntered up to the house about tea time, followed by a damp subdued little pig. I disposed of Alexander in the neighbourhood; he did fairly well when he had settled down.

Pigling Bland went on alone dejectedly; he came to crossroads and a sign-post—'To Market Town, 5 miles,' 'Over the Hills, 4 miles,' 'To Pettitoes Farm, 3 miles.'

Pigling Bland was shocked, there was little hope of sleeping in Market Town, and to-morrow was the hiring fair; it was deplorable to think how much time had been wasted by the frivolity of Alexander.

He glanced wistfully along the road towards the hills, and then set off walking obediently the other way, buttoning up his coat against the rain. He had never wanted to go; and the idea of standing all by himself in a crowded market, to be stared at, pushed, and hired by some big strange farmer was very disagreeable—

'I wish I could have a little garden and grow potatoes,' said Pigling Bland.

He put his cold hand in his pocket and felt his paper, he put his other hand in his other pocket and felt another paper—Alexander's! Pigling squealed; then ran back frantically, hoping to overtake Alexander and the policeman.

He took a wrong turn—several wrong turns, and was quite lost.

It grew dark, the wind whistled, the trees creaked and groaned.

Pigling Bland became frightened and cried 'Wee, wee, wee! I can't find my way home!'

After an hour's wandering he got out of the wood; the moon shone through the clouds, and Pigling Bland saw a country that was new to him.

The road crossed a moor; below was a wide valley with a river twinkling in the moonlight, and beyond, in misty distance, lay the hills.

He saw a small wooden hut, made his way to it, and crept inside—'I am afraid it *is* a hen house, but what can I do?' said Pigling Bland, wet and cold and quite tired out.

'Bacon and eggs, bacon and eggs!' clucked a hen on a perch.

'Trap, trap, trap! cackle, cackle, cackle!' scolded the disturbed cockerel. 'To market, to market! jiggetty jig!' clucked a broody white hen roosting next to him. Pigling Bland, much alarmed, determined to leave at daybreak. In the meantime, he and the hens fell asleep.

In less than an hour they were all awakened. The owner, Mr. Peter Thomas Piperson, came with a lantern and a hamper to catch six fowls to take to market in the morning.

He grabbed the white hen roosting next to the cock; then his eye fell upon Pigling Bland, squeezed up in a corner. He made a singular remark—'Hallo, here's another!'—seized Pigling by the scruff of the neck, and dropped him into the hamper. Then he dropped in five more dirty, kicking, cackling hens upon the top of Pigling Bland.

The hamper containing six fowls and a young pig was no light weight; it was taken down hill, unsteadily, with jerks. Pigling, although nearly scratched to pieces, contrived to hide the papers and peppermints inside his clothes.

At last the hamper was bumped down upon a kitchen floor, the lid was opened, and Pigling was lifted out. He looked up, blinking, and saw an offensively ugly elderly man, grinning from ear to ear.

'This one's come of himself, whatever,' said Mr. Piperson, turning Pigling's pockets inside out. He pushed the hamper into a corner, threw a sack over it to keep the hens quiet, put a pot on the fire, and unlaced his boots.

Pigling Bland drew forward a coppy stool, and sat on the edge of it, shyly warming his hands. Mr. Piperson pulled off a boot and threw it against the wainscot at the further end of the kitchen. There was a smothered noise—'Shut up!' said Mr. Piperson. Pigling Bland warmed his hands, and eyed him.

Mr. Piperson pulled off the other boot and flung it after the first, there was again a curious noise—'Be quiet, will ye?' said Mr. Piperson. Pigling Bland sat on the very edge of the coppy stool.

Mr. Piperson fetched meal from a chest and made porridge. It seemed to Pigling that something at the further end of the kitchen was taking a suppressed interest in the cooking, but he was too hungry to be troubled by noises.

Mr. Piperson poured out three platefuls: for himself, for Pigling, and a third—after glaring at Pigling—he put away with much scuffling, and locked up. Pigling Bland ate his supper discreetly.

After supper Mr. Piperson consulted an almanac, and felt Pigling's ribs; it was too late in the season for curing bacon, and he grudged his meal. Besides, the hens had seen this pig.

He looked at the small remains of a flitch, and then looked undecidedly at Pigling. 'You may sleep on the rug,' said Mr. Peter Thomas Piperson.

Pigling Bland slept like a top. In the morning Mr. Piperson made more porridge; the weather was warmer. He looked to see how much meal was left in the chest, and seemed dissatisfied—'You'll likely be moving on again?' said he to Pigling Bland.

Before Pigling could reply, a neighbour, who was giving Mr. Piperson and the hens a lift, whistled from the gate. Mr. Piperson hurried out with the hamper, enjoining Pigling to shut the door behind him and not meddle with nought; or 'I'll come back and skin ye!' said Mr. Piperson.

It crossed Pigling's mind that if *he* had asked for a lift, too, he might still have been in time for market.

But he distrusted Peter Thomas.

After finishing breakfast at his leisure, Pigling had a look round the cottage; everything was locked up. He found some potato peelings in a bucket in the back kitchen. Pigling ate the peel, and washed up the porridge plates in the bucket. He sang while he worked—

'Tom with his pipe made such a noise,
    He called up all the girls and boys—
'And they all ran to hear him play
    '"Over the hills and far away!"'

Suddenly a little smothered voice chimed in—

'Over the hills and a great way off,
    The wind shall blow my top knot off!'

Pigling Bland put down a plate which he was wiping, and listened.

After a long pause, Pigling went on tip-toe and peeped round the door into the front kitchen. There was nobody there.

After a long pause, Pigling went on tip-toe and peeped round the door into the front kitchen. There was nobody there.

After another pause, Pigling approached the door of the locked cupboard, and snuffed at the keyhole. It was quite quiet.

After another long pause, Pigling pushed a peppermint under the door. It was sucked in immediately.

In the course of the day Pigling pushed in all the remaining six peppermints.

When Mr. Piperson returned, he found Pigling sitting before the fire; he had brushed up the hearth and put on the pot to boil; the meal was not get-at-able.

Mr. Piperson was very affable; he slapped Pigling on the back, made lots of porridge and forgot to lock the meal chest. He did lock the cupboard door; but without properly shutting it. He went to bed early, and told Pigling upon no account to disturb him next day before twelve o'clock.

Pigling Bland sat by the fire, eating his supper.

All at once at his elbow, a little voice spoke—'My name is Pig-wig. Make me more porridge, please!' Pigling Bland jumped, and looked round.

A perfectly lovely little black Berkshire pig stood smiling beside him. She had twinkly little screwed up eyes, a double chin, and a short turned up nose.

She pointed at Pigling's plate; he hastily gave it to her, and fled to the meal chest. 'How did you come here?' asked Pigling Bland.

'Stolen,' replied Pig-wig, with her mouth full. Pigling helped himself to meal without scruple. 'What for?' 'Bacon, hams,' replied Pig-wig cheerfully. 'Why on earth don't you run away?' exclaimed the horrified Pigling.

'I shall after supper,' said Pig-wig decidedly.
Pigling Bland made more porridge and watched her shyly.

She finished a second plate, got up, and looked about her, as though she were going to start.

'You can't go in the dark,' said Pigling Bland.

Pig-wig looked anxious.

'Do you know your way by daylight?'

'I know we can see this little white house from the hills across the river. Which way are *you* going, Mr. Pig?'

'To market—I have two pig papers. I might take you to the bridge; if you have no objection,' said Pigling much confused and sitting on the edge of his coppy stool. Pig-wig's gratitude was such and she asked so many questions that it became embarrassing to Pigling Bland.

He was obliged to shut his eyes and pretend to sleep. She became quiet, and there was a smell of peppermint.

'I thought you had eaten them,' said Pigling, waking suddenly.

'Only the corners,' replied Pig-wig, studying the sentiments with much interest by the firelight.

'I wish you wouldn't; he might smell them through the ceiling,' said the alarmed Pigling.

Pig-wig put back the sticky peppermints into her pocket; 'Sing something,' she demanded.

'I am sorry ... I have toothache,' said Pigling much dismayed. 'Then I will sing,' replied Pig-wig. 'You will not mind if I say iddy tidditty? I have forgotten some of the words.'

Pigling Bland made no objection; he sat with his eyes half shut, and watched her.

She wagged her head and rocked about, clapping time and singing in a sweet little grunty voice—

'A funny old mother pig lived in a stye, and three little piggies had she;
'(Ti idditty idditty) umph, umph, umph! and the little pigs said, wee, wee!'

She sang successfully through three or four verses, only at every verse her head nodded a little lower, and her little twinkly eyes closed up.

'Those three little piggies grew peaky and lean, and lean they might very well be;
'For somehow they couldn't say umph, umph, umph! and they wouldn't say wee, wee, wee!
'For somehow they couldn't say—

Pig-wig's head bobbed lower and lower, until she rolled over, a little round ball, fast asleep on the hearth-rug.

Pigling Bland, on tip-toe, covered her up with an anti-macassar.

He was afraid to go to sleep himself; for the rest of the night he sat listening to the chirping of the crickets and to the snores of Mr. Piperson overhead.

Early in the morning, between dark and daylight, Pigling tied up his little bundle and woke up Pigwig. She was excited and half-frightened.

'But it's dark! How can we find our way?'

'The cock has crowed; we must start before the hens come out; they might shout to Mr. Piperson.'

Pig-wig sat down again, and commenced to cry.

'Come away Pig-wig; we can see when we get used to it. Come! I can hear them clucking!'

Pigling had never said shuh! to a hen in his life, being peaceable; also he remembered the hamper.

He opened the house door quietly and shut it after them. There was no garden; the neighbourhood of Mr. Piperson's was all scratched up by fowls. They slipped away hand in hand across an untidy field to the road.

The sun rose while they were crossing the moor, a dazzle of light over the tops of the hills. The sunshine crept down the slopes into the peaceful green valleys, where little white cottages nestled in gardens and orchards.

'That's Westmorland,' said Pig-wig. She dropped Pigling's hand and commenced to dance, singing—

'Tom, Tom, the piper's son, stole a pig
  and away he ran!
'But all the tune that he could play,
  was "Over the hills and far away!"'

'Come, Pig-wig, we must get to the bridge before folks are stirring.' 'Why do you want to go to market, Pigling?' inquired Pig-wig presently. 'I don't want; I want to grow potatoes.' 'Have a peppermint?' said Pig-wig. Pigling Bland refused quite crossly. 'Does your poor toothy hurt?' inquired Pig-wig. Pigling Bland grunted.

Pig-wig ate the peppermint herself and followed the opposite side of the road. 'Pig-wig! keep under the wall, there's a man ploughing.' Pig-wig crossed over, they hurried down hill towards the county boundary.

Suddenly Pigling stopped; he heard wheels.

Slowly jogging up the road below them came a tradesman's cart. The reins flapped on the horse's back, the grocer was reading a newspaper.

'Take that peppermint out of your mouth, Pig-wig, we may have to run. Don't say one word. Leave it to me. And in sight of the bridge!' said poor Pigling, nearly crying. He began to walk frightfully lame, holding Pig-wig's arm.

The grocer, intent upon his newspaper, might have passed them, if his horse had not shied and snorted. He pulled the cart crossways, and held down his whip. 'Hallo! Where are *you* going to?'—Pigling Bland stared at him vacantly.

'Are you deaf? Are you going to market?' Pigling nodded slowly.

'I thought as much. It was yesterday. Show me your licence?'

Pigling stared at the off hind shoe of the grocer's horse which had picked up a stone.

The grocer flicked his whip—'Papers? Pig licence?' Pigling fumbled in all his pockets, and handed up the papers. The grocer read them, but still seemed dissatisfied. 'This here pig is a young lady; is her name Alexander?' Pig-wig opened her mouth and shut it again; Pigling coughed asthmatically.

The grocer ran his finger down the advertisement column of his newspaper—'Lost, stolen or strayed, 10s. reward.' He looked suspiciously at Pig-wig. Then he stood up in the trap, and whistled for the ploughman.

'You wait here while I drive on and speak to him,' said the grocer, gathering up the reins. He knew that pigs are slippery; but surely, such a *very* lame pig could never run!

'Not yet, Pig-wig, he will look back.' The grocer did so; he saw the two pigs stock-still in the middle of the road. Then he looked over at his horse's heels; it was lame also; the stone took some time to knock out, after he got to the ploughman.

'Now, Pig-wig. NOW!' said Pigling Bland.

Never did any pigs run as these pigs ran! They raced and squealed and pelted down the long white hill towards the bridge. Little fat Pig-wig's petticoats fluttered, and her feet went pitter, patter, pitter, as she bounded and jumped.

They ran, and they ran, and they ran down the hill, and across a short cut on level green turf at the bottom, between pebble beds and rushes.

They came to the river, they came to the bridge—they crossed it hand in hand—then over the hills and far away she danced with Pigling Bland!

The "PETER RABBIT" BOOKS
by BEATRIX POTTER

PETER RABBIT · SQUIRREL NUTKIN
TAILOR OF GLOUCESTER · BENJAMIN BUNNY
TWO BAD MICE · MRS. TIGGY – WINKLE
MR. JEREMY FISHER · TOM KITTEN
JEMIMA PUDDLE-DUCK · THE FLOPSY BUNNIES
MRS. TITTLEMOUSE · TIMMY TIPTOES
JOHNNY TOWN-MOUSE · MR. TOD
PIGLING BLAND · SAMUEL WHISKERS
THE PIE & THE PATTY-PAN · GINGER & PICKLES
LITTLE PIG ROBINSON

A FIERCE BAD RABBIT   MISS MOPPET
APPLEY DAPPLY'S   CECILY PARSLEY'S
  NURSERY RHYMES   NURSERY RHYMES
    PETER RABBIT'S   TOM KITTEN'S
      PAINTING BOOK   PAINTING BOOK